Autumn Gold

Welcome to Woodsburrow

Book One

J. R. Cook

First paperback edition January 2024

ISBN 979-8-9898991-0-4 (paperback edition) 979-8-9898991-1-1 (eBook edition)

To my husband, who makes me believe that anything is possible.

Chapter 1

An email. A nonpersonal, generic best of luck to you email was how her company of 5 years decided to tell the unlucky seventy-six people they were getting laid off. Jovi couldn't understand how two months ago her review called her an "outstanding employee" and "very valuable to the team," and today she was an easy way to save the company from going broke. Her mind was racing, her chest felt tight, and she started to feel detached, empty. At least it was the end of the day. She needed to get out of there.

Jovi unlocked the creaky door to her apartment and threw her stuff down on the plain, white countertops in her very white kitchen. The loud clunk seemed to echo off the walls. The colors, or lack of, felt blinding and sterile today. This place felt no more comforting than the office had. She needed a run, or a drink. She would get both tonight. Jovi had a date with Dylan like they did every Tuesday night. What would he say about the lay off? Instead of feeling solace, she felt uneasy. Dylan was a successful attorney at a high-powered law firm. He valued success and "grinding" as he called it. Well, she had "grinded" for the last five years, and she was still expendable. "Grinding" hadn't set her apart, and there were thousands of people just like her that her company, or any other, could add and subtract when it suited them.

She laced up her favorite running shoes and pulled on a wind jacket. It had started to rain outside, a chilling spring rain that pelted her skin like rocks as she left the building. She ran the same path every evening starting at her apartment. She followed the winding streets to the local park, and back. The movement helped clear her mind. It made her feel alive, something she didn't feel at her job even on a good day. "If only my life was this easy to fix." Jovi muttered. She got back into the apartment and stripped off her wet clothes that were plastered to her body. She hurried to get into the warm shower before her date.

Jovi pulled into the parking lot of Figaro's a few hours later. A drive that was only a few miles had taken a ridiculous thirty minutes from all the traffic. Traffic in the city usually didn't bother her, but it felt like salt on a wound today. Jovi left her car and blocked the rain almost comically with her hand while she ran to the entrance of the restaurant. She wiped the drops that had started to fall down her face and looked up to see Dylan at a table by the window. His eyes were glued to his phone. He didn't even look up when she sat down.

"Hi Dylan." Jovi greeted him.

"Jovi." He nodded his head and proceed to finish whatever junk he was reading. When he was done, he talked on and on about the recent case he was assigned.

Jovi didn't mind listening to it. In fact, Dylan was a great storyteller who pulled in your attention. It was one of his traits that made him an excellent lawyer. When Jovi finished her entrée, she realized Dylan hadn't asked her a single question about herself. He hadn't paused long enough for her to share anything without prompting either. When she started to speak, Dylan immediately interrupted her.

"Listen Jovi." He began, "These last six months have been fun, but I just can't dedicate the time to this relationship anymore. You are a nice girl, but I don't think we should waste time with each other any longer."

Was he serious? She thought. *Waste time with me?* All this man did was listen to the sound of his own voice. After six months of events, dates, sex, and she was a waste of time. "You can't be serious." She said. "You think I'm a waste of time? All I've been doing the last six months is listening to you talk!" She shouted. "What do you even know about me that you can put off such a judgement?"

He shrugged. "All the more reason for us not to continue this arrangement anymore. And to be frank, I've started seeing Izzy. She has more depth, and a vibrance for life."

"Izzy the intern?"

He nodded. "So anyway, good luck." He took the bill and walked up to the bar to pay. Jovi drained her large glass of Zin and headed for the door.

As she slid into her driver's seat, she sat as her car warmed up. The tears started to flow. She hadn't expected a marriage proposal, and Dylan might be the most self-centered person she had ever met, but he was handsome and the third relationship in a row that she had been the one dumped. Jovi thought of what he had said of Izzy's vibrance for life.

Jovi's life had felt dull and colorless in a sedated way for years now. The city was dirty and cold. It was always noisy in the loneliest way. There wasn't passion in her relationships, nor was there passion at work. Jovi felt in that moment, that she was the one without color dulling the world around her. She had stopped dreaming and stopped believing in the future. She went through the motions every day without much thought to them. The emptiness felt heavy. She was ugly crying now and she knew it, but she couldn't stop the stream of tears.

Jovi had come to the city looking for something other than what she had as a child. Growing up with just her mom in the suburbs had been lonely as well. Her mom worked two jobs to afford their tiny one-bedroom apartment. The kids at school laughed at her secondhand clothes. The only time she felt seen and not isolated was weekends her mom and her had spent on her grandparents' farm. They were gone now, and she missed them terribly. Her mom had married and started a new family. Jovi struggled to find her place in that family. She lacked connection and her place in the city as well. Now she was here, crying in an empty parking lot.

Returning home, she took a long hot shower. She scrubbed her skin furiously trying to wash the day off. When she finally steadied her breathing, she got out and found her oldest frumpiest sweatpants and long soft socks. She put on her big baggy "Go Bulldogs!" college sweatshirt and grabbed the mint chocolate chip ice cream from the freezer. "There isn't anything I can do to save this day from being horrible. Tomorrow is a new day. Tomorrow is a new day." She repeated to herself.

The next day, the rain had at least stopped. She went to work but found herself distracted and daydreaming. She had done some job scans, but she didn't have a clue what she might want to do next. She asked herself for the first time, do I even like this? She looked around at her workspace. She had a picture of her mom and her from last Christmas, a calendar of beautiful pictures from around the state she had picked up at a local craft fair, and her coffee cup with a corny "Dream big" written on it, a gag gift from the office gift exchange. She wasn't sure she was happy and couldn't think of a day in recent months when she had been.

And where were the girlfriends she was supposed to have? After being the poor kid in high school, she didn't retain any significant friendships from that time in her life. In college, her roommate had been her best friend, until she started sleeping with Jovi's boyfriend at the time. Those two snuck around her for weeks. Neither had the courage nor possessed enough honesty to tell her the truth. She was pretty sure they were married with kids now. That had happened at the end of senior year. So, she left college with mostly friendly acquaintances. She had met people she enjoyed at her job when she first moved into town. They used to get drinks after work, laugh and tell each other intimate secrets, but they had all moved onto another job or had kids and stayed home. She had learned by now that "stay in touch" was much easier to say that to actually do.

So here she was, with no one to call after having the absolute worst day. A barren apartment to go home to, and a job that sucked most of her time and energy but didn't fuel any type of passion. She had two meetings left for the day, and she counted down every minute of the last hour.

She arrived home that evening and noticed there was a white envelope taped to her front door. She looked down the hall to her left and right in an automatic response. Every apartment had the same envelope. Her heart sank. Jovi tore it open. The owners were selling the complex, and she was being asked to leave. That left her with no home, no job, no boyfriend, no friends, and no light for the life she was living. It was time to move on, but she did not have a clue where to start.

When she finished her run that evening, she pulled out some leftover Chinese and took her cold fried rice and phone to the couch. After some scrolling and searching, she decided what she needed was a few days away. When was the last time she had taken time off? It had been a while. Her PTO bank was probably maxed out. Jovi was not about to go through the motions again tomorrow. She really thought about the last time she had been full of life and connected to her surroundings. Her mind wandered to the little lake town she had spent a Fourth of July at in college. *What was the name of it, Woodville? No, that wasn't it. Woodsburrow!* She searched the town on the Airbnb website and booked a place for the rest of the week. She would get some space, some air, and she would try to figure out where on Earth she took this wrong turn and which path she belonged on next.

That night when she laid down, she considered what may be the next step in her future. She hadn't done much besides work, run, and casually date since graduation. She had done well at her job and had been paid more than competitively. She was also going to be receiving at severance that at the very least, would cover living expenses for her basic needs through one year, maybe even longer. Between her savings she had built and the inheritance she had received from being the only grandchild of her beloved grandparents, she could do whatever it was she pleased, and live wherever she wanted. Maybe she needed a change of scenery? She could move. She had thought about Seattle, and New Orleans in the past. Cities that had unique personalities and plenty to do.

No doubt there would be ample job opportunities at either location.

As she slept that evening, she dreamt of open spaces and warm sun. She was immersed in a cozy home with smells of fresh bread baking and birds singing. She was there in a simple, slower life rich in history and strong community. Although she saw no faces, she knew there were people around her who loved her and were there or would be there if she opened her mouth and called them. She felt rooted down firmly in the place she was, and it was the happiest feeling she could imagine.

In the morning, the sun was shining. She had sent her manager a message that morning letting her know she wouldn't be back in the office until Monday. She felt the tension drain out of her. Jovi packed for her trip as she slowly sipped her coffee. She had picked up the habit of drinking it black at the office. People had made a big deal about drinking it in its purest form. Between the diets and the talk of not drowning the flavor, that became the only way that it was drank. She realized this morning that she hated black coffee. Why had she been consuming it in a way she didn't like? She took out her milk and sugar and added it to her cup. It was glorious. Now was the time to explore herself. She was starting here. She took another sip and sighed, heaven in a cup.

She packed a huge variety of clothes. You never knew what to expect during spring weather. Some days felt like summer, and the next like the dead of winter, and sometimes that was all in the same 24-hour period. She didn't know what time it was when she loaded up her Subaru, but it felt good not to actually care.

<u>*Chapter 2*</u>

Woodsburrow was a sleepy little town this time of year. It was 2 hours north of the city and off the beaten path. Most of the tourism came during the summer and fall months. "This looks right out of a postcard." She gasped as she looked around at the downtown. The city lamp posts were still wrapped with green garland. There was a library in a giant old building, a family own grocery store, a little diner (The Cozy Kitchen), and a sweet little bakery. The Main Street continued with businesses that were all locally owned. There were no chains here, and she didn't think any would be welcome. People were talking to each other on the street without any cellphones in sight. In the city, people walked down the street without glancing up at the next person, completely engrossed in their phones but blind to the world around them.

Her Airbnb was a cozy cottage north of town. Jovi could see Lost Lake from the giant sprawling living room window. The lake was calm as glass. All around the lake, the grass had not started to turn green just yet, but little patches of wildflowers were beginning to grow with blazes of pink and purple doting the surrounding patches of lawns. Giant trees encircled the lake and continued as far as she could see.

Jovi decided she would put on her running clothes and explore almost immediately after unpacking. There were trails that wrapped around the lake through the woods. She couldn't think of a more peaceful place. As she ran, the tension from the week left her shoulders. Her breath felt larger and her mind felt at ease. Being outdoors had always given her a sense of peace. It was in the sounds of only nature around her, no cars, or trains or that constant hum the city always possessed. She heard the branches swaying in the wind as the breeze began to build. The chickadees and mourning doves with their chirping and cooing followed her to a creek. She heard the water running past her in a fluid motion down towards the lake. She stopped and closed her eyes. Her breath continued to heave, but she felt calm. Wet feet and sweaty hair graced her body. She felt alive like she had awakened something inside her that had long been asleep.

She took a trail that followed the creek and somehow ended up on a road. Jovi went with it. It seemed like no one had been in this direction recently and that felt empowering. She saw an old Victorian home with huge oak and maple trees in the front yard. A forest of ancient pines and birch led the way to the stately home. As she got closer to the driveway, she began to see the shape of a sign in the yard. No cars were in the driveway nor were there tire tracks in the muddy drive.

When she stopped directly in front of the house, she gasped. There was a giant overgrown garden behind the home, no doubt an old kitchen and herb garden. The front flower beds had the start of erupting tulips and daffodils. Farther back behind the house to the right, was an old orchard. She could see hundreds of large trees from here. There was a beautiful weathered, but well-maintained barn as well that sat near the orchard at the end of the driveway. This place was stunning. The character of it all absolutely spoke to Jovi's soul. It made her feel like she had found a kindred spirit. She felt like she had been here before, and what's more, like she belonged.

She looked down, remembering the sign she had noticed. It was a for sale sign. In that moment, it was as if she had been transported straight into her dream. She didn't remember the details, but the feeling still burned strongly. She tried to remember again why she had thought the city suited her. For the life of her, she couldn't. Had she really settled there just for the job? Had she gone through the motions of the hustle and bustle because she felt that was expected of her, like that was the only way to achieve happiness? Her mother had never insinuated that. She had wanted her to pursue a full life but had never dictated to her how that should look. Her mother was an artist, a feeler and Jovi pursed a practical life thinking that would be a safer choice. Standing there in front of this house that held its own history, character, and unique energy, she felt bonded. She saw the potential in the magnificent orchard. She could see herself spending her days tending to the trees. She could feel the enchantment of fall, and the rush of people visiting for their own piece of it. She felt it rise in her chest, the feeling of home. Was she willing to take such a large risk? Was she ready to plant roots that deep?

After she returned to the cottage. She felt renewed. She stretched while looking at the lake and watched the different ducks and waterfowl. She hadn't stopped to observe the world in a long while and she sat transfixed by their simple movements. After a few hours had passed, Jovi decided to take a trip into town to pick up some groceries for her stay. She was thankful to have a kitchen to prepare her meals in. Although going out to eat was enjoyable, she loved to cook.

She passed a hardware store, the local school, and an apothecary. *Was this place for real?* Jovi parked and went inside the grocery store. There were little old ladies catching up on gossip, and moms with young kids who seemed overenthusiastic to be picking up groceries. Everyone said hello and smiled when they passed. She did the same.

Jovi gathered her items and headed to the check-out. As she turned around, double checking her mental list one last time, she ran right into a very tall man with dark hair and piercing green eyes. His groceries went flying in all directions. "Oops! Excuse me. I'm so sorry. I wasn't paying close enough attention to where I was going." Her cheeks burned crimson as she looked up.

The man answered, "It's ok, really. It's probably my fault anyway. I looked down and saw my phone was ringing and here we are." He shrugged. "No permanent harm was done. My name is Steele. I don't think I've seen you around before." His voice was friendly and warm as he reached out to shake her hand, and they both bent down to collect the fallen items. They collided again as they got down to the ground. He smiled a genuine smile, and they laughed.

"No, you haven't." Jovi replied still giggling. "I'm just here visiting for the week. I can't get over the charm this town has. My name is Jovi." Her hands felt hot and clammy immediately as she shook his large strong hand. She quickly removed her hand like she had been burned by the touch and swiped at a hair in front of her eyes.

"You should come to the Firelight Festival Saturday evening. The proceeds go to our Ice organization. We maintain the rink for ice skating, hockey, curling, open skate, and various other groups. It has ice sculpting and food trucks, different artisan vendors, hot chocolate, live music, and a bonfire. If you want to see Woodsburrow's charm on full blast, it's the place to be."

"That sounds really wonderful. I'll consider it." Jovi replied.

"It was nice meeting you. I have to return this call." He said shaking his cell phone in his hand. "Don't be a stranger if you see me again." He said.

Jovi smiled feeling more at ease with the new friendly face. "I won't."

The cashier was just as friendly as everyone else in the store had been. She slipped a flier for the Firelight Festival that Steele had mentioned into her grocery bags. Apparently, this Festival was a big deal. Jovi grabbed her bag and headed out the front door. When she threw the bag in her backseat, the smell of hot yeast and sugar permeated her nose. This week was all about exploring her likes, so she promptly followed the smell. She crossed the street to the bakery.

Chapter 3

Drury Lane was a brick building with old accent lumber pieces that ran the length of the ceiling. The inside had a warm eclectic feel. Bright colors decorated the walls, and the lighting was soft. As she entered, she could hear a woman singing. The song stopped, and she heard, "I'll be right with you." That came from far in the back.

"No problem. I'll just browse. That scent is intoxicating!" Jovi closed her eyes and took a deep inhale. Although she enjoyed cooking, she had never done much baking. Baking was about sharing joy with others, and she didn't have those people in her life she could shower with goodies.

A stunning blonde with a cheery and inviting demeanor entered. She had powdered sugar on her shirt, and she carried a tray overfilled with baked goods. "If you want intoxicating you need to try these." She handed Jovi a square that looked like a flakey pie crust topped with a white sweet cheese and a reddish green fruit mix. Powdered sugar was dusted on the top. "It's rhubarb cherry tart." She said as Jovi made a moaning noise with her first bite. The light flakey crunch was followed by a decadent richness and ended with tart mixed with sweet. The balance was incredible.

"This is the best thing I've ever eaten." She smiled at the woman.

"It's a new menu item." The woman winked at her. "I'm Hannah. Welcome to my shop."

Jovi looked around. "This place is yours? I would never eat another real meal if I owned this."

Hannah laughed. "It's pretty great, and I do still manage to get out and eat some veggies. Are you new here?" She asked, watching attentively for Jovi's reply.

"Just visiting, but after eating this I might consider full time residency! I'm Jovi."

"Well Jovi, it's nice to meet you. Can I get you anything?"

Jovi looked over at the cases of goodies and decided on maple sugar cookies shaped like maple leaves and colored with a royal icing that matched their fall color perfectly, strawberry lemonade scones with pink frosting, and a half-sized loaf of sourdough bread.

As she looked over the items, they chatted like old friends. Hannah had moved from the city after getting burnt out as a pastry chef working with the top baker's in the state. She decided she was tired of chasing someone else's vision, and it was time to chase her own. "I love that you run your own business. You are obviously way too talented to be hidden behind someone else's name."

Hannah smiled. "I love baking. I couldn't imagine doing anything else. The regular customers I get here are more like family than the regulars back in the city. All summer long I get the tourist population, but they are happy to get anything fresh. They aren't coming in berating you for some kind of order imperfection like the wrong shade of chartreuse."

Jovi nodded. "The people are so different here, and I love it. There is more room to breathe and more space. You don't feel so claustrophobic all the time."

Hannah cocked her head to the side "Do you have a boyfriend?"

Jovi shook her head no.

"A career you love?"

Jovi shook her head again.

"Then what the heck are you doing in the city when you clearly hate it!" Hannah said.

"I don't know that I hate it..." Jovi responded.

"You do." Hannah said. "I've known you for twenty minutes, and it's obvious to me! It's not to you?" She asked.

Jovi paused. "You may be right. I've had a really rough week, and I feel like I'm seeing my life through a completely different lens."

Jovi didn't know what it was about Hannah, but immediately they both felt that they were supposed to be friends. Hannah genuinely listened to Jovi. Jovi shared things with her she normally wouldn't have said out loud to anyone. She told her all about the layoff and the breakup.

"What an ass! You definitely need something with chocolate." She said as she handed her a chocolate brownie square.

"He was." Jovi agreed with a huge mouthful. She swallowed. "But the worst part is, I didn't even like him. Why did I keep dating someone like that? There was never any spark. He was just someone to fill my Tuesday nights with. The sex was quick and unmemorable. I've never been with someone who was interesting for more than a few dates."

"That was the same with me until I met Luke." Hannah said. "When I moved to town, he came in every morning for a cinnamon roll and chocolate chip cookie. It took me weeks to realize he wasn't actually coming for baked goods, and that I was waiting for him to show up every morning. I was so shocked anyone would spend that much time getting to know me before even taking me out. He has been my safe space for the last year now and nothing about our chemistry is boring." Hannah smiled. "We just got engaged this Christmas actually!" Hannah exclaimed and showed off her sparkly stone. "He honestly makes everything in life just a little richer. But the number of frogs I had to kiss to get here, is a little ridiculous."

Hannah looked at the clock. "It's time for me to lock up." She looked at Jovi. "I open the bakery tomorrow, and Marg comes in to watch the counter for the day. Do you want to grab lunch at the Cozy Kitchen? I could be there at oneish. I can continue to persuade you to leave the city." Hannah smiled.

"That sounds great." Jovi replied. "One will work fine." This town was wrapping around her like an old quilt, soft and worn with age, and so warm you never wanted to move from under it again.

Jovi returned to the cottage as the cotton candy sunset was spreading its comforting orange and pink hues over the sky. The lake was a perfect mirrored image of the magnificent masterpiece. Although the darkness that trickled in brought cold air with it, Jovi opened a window to listen to the frog's chirp as she chopped potatoes and leeks for her stew. She preheated the oven to warm

Hannah's bread and poured herself a glass of wine. She could imagine the olden hidden house, and the rows upon rows of apple trees on the hill.

As a child, her mom had done her best to make magic for her despite their lack of funds. She had taken her to an orchard a few times, and Jovi had thought it was the most enchanted place. She could not believe the rows of plain looking trees had grown apples. You might as well have said "abracadabra" and waved a wand.

She hadn't thought of those memories for years. As a child she had played life safe and on the sidelines. All she wanted was to blend in with the crowd. She never wanted attention drawn to herself. Being a poor illegitimate child without a father brought no good remarks when conversations shifted to her. She did not want to be labeled a victim. She just wanted to be left alone. After all, she knew no other way of life. She didn't really know what she had been missing so she had no idea she should feel like she was missing something. Somewhere along the line, her trying to blend in, turned into her no longer dreaming for herself. Did she want to own an orchard? Could she? She needed to start believing in her own ability to foster her dreams into a reality. If she continued to avoid dreaming, she would live out her numbing existence she had been living thus far. She didn't need to be invisible anymore nor did she need to live a life that looked like anyone else's.

The following day was Friday. When Jovi woke to the chorus of various birds, she slowly opened her eyes. She took a minute to consider the decision she had made last night. She tried to determine if she was thinking irrationally. She thought about how she might feel about the choice months from now or even years. Would there be regret? She thought about different jobs she could apply for in the city, other cities she had considered in the past a possible future adventure. What did she want?

Her phone rang. She was so deep in thought, and so caught up in the ambiance of the lake that it might as well have been a burglar alarm. She grabbed it hastily and looked at the screen. It was her mom. "Hi, Mom." Jovi answered.

"Sorry to bother you at work, Sweetie." Her mom said.

"No bother, Mom. I actually took a few days and went out of town." "Some alone time with that Dylan? Is it getting serious? Do you think we will meet this one?" Her mother asked. She never took trips with her previous partners. It just never reached that commitment level, whatever level you could call a planned overnight trip.

"No Mom, actually we aren't together anymore." Jovi exhaled.

"Oh Jovi, that's too bad. I know you liked him."

"It's ok Mom." Jovi countered. "Really. He was way too full of himself. I think it might be for the best."

"Well speaking of good things, I wanted to call to let you know first. I'm pregnant."

"Pregnant? You are? Aren't you too old for that?" Jovi quickly regretted that comment, but really? Her mom was living a better life than the one they had lived. It was like she got a complete do over. Jovi was left trying to piece together life for herself.

"Thank you for reminding me that I'll be labeled a geriatric pregnancy for the next eight months." Her mother groaned.

"Not that you are old Mom. I just didn't know you and David wanted more kids after Silas." Her brother was three, and that felt weird. She had coworkers her age with three-year-olds. She couldn't even keep a boyfriend.

"Well," she said. "It's rare to get pregnant naturally at 45. We haven't been preventing due to how unlikely it is. It's a blessing to be given another child, Jovi. You will feel that one day. Enjoy your vacation and come visit when you get back. Silas would love to see you, and so would I."

"OK Mom. I will." Jovi sighed. "Love you."

"Love you too, honey."

They hung up.

Her mom was pregnant again. *Well, hadn't she suffered enough raising her alone?* David took amazing care of her mom and treated her like a queen. He was a bit younger than her, but he loved her artistic flair and free soul. Jovi was grown when they met, so he was not a father figure to her, but she liked him well enough. And Silas was actually a cool kid. He loved dinosaurs and outer space and lit up like a Christmas tree every time Jovi visited. Her mom was living her dream. It was time for Jovi to chase one of her own.

<u>Chapter 4</u>

Jovi dialed the number for the realtor's office she had passed downtown. She spoke to a woman named Shannon, and they made an appointment for 10:00 at the hidden house. Jovi pulled out her warmest sweater and insulated leggings paired with her oversized boots. It was supposed to be the chilliest day this week, but she was determined to see every bit of that property without the weather stopping her.

Shannon met Jovi at the end of the driveway and greeted her. "Hi there! I'm Shannon. I'm so excited you asked to see Lynn's place. The estate holder is anxious to get it sold."

"Thank you for having time for me on such short notice. It is such a charming place." *So, this place had been owned by a woman who had no family.* Shannon led the way up the wet driveway to the large front porch. Jovi dodged puddles and took in the view. It was so quiet. Jovi knew there wasn't anyone around for miles. She heard the rustle of the big trees. The wind blew the clouds out of the sun's way, and sun beams warmed her face only increasing that feeling of home that was washing over her. The back porch was amazing. The view of the orchard on the hill was its center point.

She looked over the porch and noted the boards were in excellent condition. This place had been well loved by the woman who had lived here before. Shannon found the key and unlocked the front door. As Jovi entered the home, the colors, trims, light fixtures, and flooring could not have been more different than her grey and white apartment she had called home for years, and she absolutely loved it. The richness and dark hues, the bold wallpaper, the fireplace that was the center piece of the living room was all exactly how she had pictured it would be and more. "Is the fireplace functional?" Jovi asked.

"Yes." Shannon replied. "Lynn used the fireplace last fall before she passed. Her estate holder had it inspected to ensure all was up to par for the sale."

There were beautiful built-in bookshelves that surrounded the fireplace. Lynn had obviously been a reader like Jovi was. Her gaze shifted to the tall ceilings and towering windows that were letting in the perfect amount of early morning sunlight.

"Lynn spent plenty of time in her kitchen baking with the apples from the orchard. It's my favorite room in the house." Shannon was saying as they rounded the corner into the kitchen. Lynn had made the perfect kitchen. There was a double oven and an oversized island in the middle. There were views from the sink into the kitchen garden. Sunbeams danced on the floor from the window.

After seeing the rest of the house, which was just as breath taking, Jovi wanted to view the outside. "The house comes with 80 acres which includes the orchard and the barn. The detached garage has one stall, but it does its job." Shannon smiled.

"I want to see the orchard if you don't mind," Jovi said.

"Not at all," said Shannon. "But I do think I will wait inside."

Jovi followed the overgrown but obvious path to the orchard. She looked around at the hundreds of well-established apple trees. A few of them looked like they needed more than some basic trimming. Some branches had fallen and cracked over the winter. There were others full of suckers and shoots. Overall, they were in great condition and planted in beautiful rows. In the back, a huge area had been cleared to continue to expand those rows. This place was it. The spirit of the trees spoke loudly to her.

✳✳✳

Jovi pulled into the parking lot of the Cozy Kitchen right as Hannah was coming down the sidewalk. Hannah waved eagerly at Jovi. Jovi got out of her Subaru and said immediately, "I'm buying a house!" Hannah shrieked and jumped up and down. She pulled Jovi into a hug. Jovi had never been much of a hugger, but this felt like the perfect moment to become one.

"Congratulations! Tell me all about it!" Hannah's spirit was infectious. She must have glowed from a mile away, but it was an inviting glow not a blinding light.

"I put in an offer for what the realtor said was Lynn Reed's place. It's stunning and has a beautiful orchard that I want to open in the fall. The offer was accepted right before I came to meet you."

"Jovi that sounds wonderful! I'd love to help. Luke works for the police department in town, but he grew up on a local family farm so if you need any heavy lifting help, he would love to show off his skills." Hannah wagged her eyebrows up and down, and Jovi laughed.

They spent the next two hours chatting like they were old friends just picking up where they left off. Jovi couldn't help but feel an overwhelming joy. They planned to meet at the Firelight Festival tomorrow. "I can't wait to meet Luke. I'm sure he is as funny and sweet as you make him sounds. You two are probably sickly perfect together." Jovi rolled her eyes and smiled.

"We are definitely sickly cute, at least that's what my sisters say. So be prepared." Hannah laughed.

When Jovi got back to the cottage, she decided to spend some time lounging. She pulled out the book she had packed and grabbed a large blanket. She laid on the couch, and that was where she fell asleep.

***

Saturday was the Firelight Festival. This would be her opportunity to meet the rest of the town. She really wanted to make a good first impression, and Jovi was nervous. She spent the day unable to sit still. She went for a long run out to her house. She gushed at it from the road. It was just as charming as it had been the first time, she saw it.

Jovi made a mental note of the things she would need for moving day and different projects she wanted to start. Although the house came partially furnished and had some older equipment, Jovi knew she would have plenty to do to keep her busy until the fall. She reluctantly said her goodbye.

Jovi was headed back to the city tomorrow to finish her final weeks before her layoff took effect. She would only get one more day to see this. She closed her eyes briefly and tried to take in everything she was feeling right now. Doubt was sure to settle in at some point. She would need this memory for strength.

It had been a warm day, the stark contrast from the day before was a perfect example of just how erratic spring weather could be. Jovi pulled on her favorite blue jeans and an emerald green t-shirt. She made sure to grab a sweatshirt before she headed out the door. She checked her reflection. Her dark curls, although unruly, were at least not full of frizz, and she had chosen a simple amount of makeup. Her mascara made her dark eyelashes striking, and the stained lip gloss plumped her lips. Jovi was a beautiful woman, the kind that didn't need pounds of make up to stick out in a crowd. Jovi wasn't aware of this of course, and as she examined her reflection; she wasn't looking for her beauty. She was looking for strength to be a small business owner, and friendliness. Jovi hoped she could engage people like Hannah did and make them feel like the words exchanged between them were the most important thing in the world at that second. She smiled at her reflection. "You can do this, Jov!" She pumped her fist in the air, and she headed out the door.

The Firelight Festival was held downtown. Although it was not getting dark quite yet, lights lit up the streets and led the way to the park at the end of the strip of businesses. She parked in front of Hannah's bakery. Jovi wasn't expecting Hannah to arrive for at least an hour, but her nervous energy had led her here early. As she opened the door of her car, the smell of spiced nuts and smokey campfires greeted her. She took a huge inhale.

Before she could even get out of her car and grab her things, she looked up and saw a man standing over her smiling obnoxiously bright. He appeared to be baring his teeth like he was on a gum commercial.

"Hi there. The name's Nick. I saw you around town. You are a beautiful woman." Nick spoke with a commanding confidence and seemed to move his eyebrows as he spoke an outlandish amount. Jovi immediately felt uneasy. She did not want to be here with this clown.

"Hi there…Nick. Umm, thank you." Jovi said with hesitation in her voice.

"We should go out on Friday." He stared at her like she was a piece of dessert. His perfectly slicked back hair and pressed clothes made him look like wax dummy. He stood closer to her than what was considered an acceptable distance, and the overwhelming cologne that he had on could probably be smelled a mile away.

She took two steps backwards. "Now is not a good time for that, Nick. Actually, I'm leaving tomorrow."

"But my intel tells me that you bought the old Reed house, so that can't be for long."

Who was this guy? Had he been stalking her? "Yes, but I won't be moving in right now. I'm not in a space I want to be dating in. Thanks anyway." Jovi tried to be clear that this conversation was over. She grabbed her bag and sweatshirt and walked hastily over to the crowd.

"Later then! I'll find you when you get back!" Nick called behind her. She groaned.

After being cornered by Nick, Jovi was eager to make distance between them and wandered over to the vendors that had set up. The first thing she did was buy some of those amazing smelling nuts. *How could you just walk past those? You would have to be insane.* Jovi thought. She walked with her nuts over to the next booth.

Grant Farms had canned goods everywhere. There were peaches, tomatoes, green beans, cherries, and hand-milled flour. The cherry pie and peach pie fillings were beautiful, brilliant colors, and tomatoes had been canned in any combination you could think of. BBQ sauce, ketchup, salsa, spaghetti sauce, pizza sauce, they had it.

"Hi there. I'm Caroline!" A spry woman in her 60's beamed at her. She looked strong and held herself with confidence.

"Hi. You guys must have a huge place to have this many different items for sale. Jovi." She said as she shook Caroline's hand.

Caroline nodded. "We do. Charlie inherited the farm from his family." She nodded towards her husband who had kind blue eyes and white hair and was unloading their truck with more goods to sell. "It had been a dairy and beef farm for years. We wanted to change it to more local commercial growing. We still do enough dairy to sell handmade cheese." She waved her hand over a table further down with artisan cheeses and a chartreuse board set out with samples. "We spend more time and acres on our fruits and vegetables. We also decided to added fruit trees like cherry, peach and plum. Autumn Gold Orchard always had the apple trees, so we didn't plant those on a commercial scale. It was so sad to see it shut down with Lynn's death. She had no family to pass it on to."

Jovi looked at her with peaked interest. "Lynn Reed?" She asked.

Caroline nodded. "We were very close friends. Did you know her?"

Jovi shook her head. "No, but I just bought her place. I want to open her orchard back up this fall and add a pumpkin patch. It's such an amazing little farm. I'd love to pick your brain sometime if you don't mind. I want to plant some new trees, so I have those popular favorites to add to her heritage varieties, but I've never planted a tree before." Caroline smiled.

"Jovi that is so beautiful that you could see all that potential without even knowing the history of it. Were you looking to buy a place?"

Jovi shook her head no. "I just stumbled on it while I was out running."

"The land is speaking to you. It's a powerful connection. Lynn had it too. Lynn used to have the best apples. She has varieties up there that taste divine. She did some roadside selling and made tons of her apple pies. They were easily the best in the county. I would plant any new trees immediately when you move in. You don't want to wait too long. I would be happy to come walk you through planting them. It really isn't hard. You will have to wait until next winter to do any pruning other than limbs that are broken off. Do you need help plowing an area for your pumpkin patch? Charlie is always looking to spend more time on his tractor." Caroline laughed.

"Yes. I didn't even think that far ahead, but you are absolutely right. I also inherited a tractor of hers and an old hay wagon. Maybe he could walk me through using them?"

Charlie had finished unloading and had joined their conversation. "Actually, we sold that old thing to Lynn years ago. We had bought all new machinery when we took over our farm. I know that tractor well. I'll give you the run down. It may need a tune up first." Charlie smiled. "You will do a great job. Most of farming comes from intuition." This man was obvious filled with patience, and Jovi felt like in that moment, he was reading her thoughts.

"I'm starting to feel like I am in over my head."

The Grants both shook their heads in disagreement. "Our country is filled with farmers and homesteaders who never came from that life. They learned what they know by doing. The land will show you what you need to know. Farming doesn't require degree or family genetics. It requires hard work and consistency, and the ability to pivot when mother nature needs you to." Charlie said. "We will help you get your feet under you." Caroline added. "Thank you, guys, so much." They exchanged numbers, and the Grants promised to be there the day after closing. They would need to promptly get her new trees and pumpkin seeds in the ground before it was too late in the season for planting.

Jovi continued down the street. She chatted with small scale jewelers and quilters. There were candle makers, painters, sculptors, potters, leatherworkers, and weavers. She couldn't believe the talent that such a small area possessed. It was such a charming event. This town felt more like home to her than she had felt anywhere since she was a child. She felt warm and happy. One of the bulging bags of items for her new house slipped out of her hand. Jovi bent to the ground and tried to arrange them steadier in the bag. She decided she would walk back to her car and meet Hannah. *It must be getting close to our meet up time.* She thought. Hours could have passed, but she wasn't sure. She definitely did not want to carry this stuff all night. As she was standing back up and turning around, she ran smack into Steele.

"We seem to be making this a regular occurrence." He laughed.

"You probably think I'm just a big klutz." Jovi frowned.

"Or maybe I'm the klutz who walks around with his head in the clouds." Steele shrugged. "You decided to come. Jovi, right? Isn't it a cool event? The bonfire is the best. The ice sculpture contest gets pretty heated, too. This time of year, winter seems to drag on. It's nice to have a part of it to look forward to before spring arrives. Do you want some help with those?" He asked.

"I was just going to bring them to my car." She replied. "You aren't leaving already, are you?" He asked urgently.

"No, I don't want to be holding them all night by the bonfire."

"I'll help." He said firmly. He reached his hand to hers to take some of her load. Their hands touched and a shock went through her body. He grabbed half the items without waiting for an answer. He walked at her side back to her car.

Every time they made eye contact; a rush swallowed her to her toes. Steele told her that he owned the hardware store in town. "My parents Charlene and Eddie ran it for years. They retired after my Dad's stroke. My brother moved into the city and manages investments. My sister is a teacher. Neither of them wanted the store, so by default I end up with it."

"Do you enjoy it?" Jovi asked. "You don't feel like you lost out on exploring your own life?"

He shrugged. "I grew up in that store. I hung out there more than my siblings ever did. I would follow my dad around and watch him interact with the customers. I pulled out different tools and parts and made towers and pretended to fix them. I used to listen to my grandpa talk with the retired men at the back counter in the mornings. They would all gather with their coffee and talk about everything from babies to farming. I love owning the store. I get to feel my family's legacy around me. Plus, my regular hours give me time to pursue life outside of it as well."

"Like what?" Jovi asked. "A family? Girlfriend? Hobbies?"

"No girlfriend or kids. I have a nephew. He is my best little buddy." He smiled. "I coach the hockey team at the high school. When I'm not doing that, I help my parents as often as I'm able, and when I have alone time, I fish."

He waved at someone further down the street. "Hey Luke!" He called.

Jovi looked up to see Hannah and Luke coming out of her shop. Hannah waved.

"Hannah!" Jovi exclaimed. Luke and Jovi were introduced and exchanged handshakes, to which Luke responded with a big bear hug. He was such a friendly guy. Hannah laughed at all his jokes. Luke was obviously absolutely smitten with Hannah because after every joke he glanced at Hannah to watch her face light up with her laughter. It was clear that Luke enjoyed being the life of the party, but he left room for Hannah to steal the show as well. Both outspoken and inviting personalities, they made everyone feel welcome.

The group of four made their way down to the bonfire. Jovi and Hannah each grabbed a hot chocolate from the concession stand, and Jovi pulled her sweatshirt over her head. The chill had arrived. At the bonfire, she looked around to see groups of people chatting. There were children playing at the playground behind them. Steele and Hannah introduced Jovi to a few people, the local salon owner, the librarian, and a schoolteacher. Luke and Steele seemed to know everyone, and everyone came up to them to say hello first. Jovi shared with anyone she could about opening the orchard and pumpkin patch this fall. She figured word of mouth was clearly the superior form of communication in this town.

"You're staying?" Steele asked uncertainly as he looked at her.

Was he disappointed? Jovi wondered. "Yes. I'll be back at the end of May, for good."

Steele seemed to become quiet after that. Jovi thought he tried to avoid making eye contact with her. *And was that salon owner looking at him a little obsessively?*

Eventually, Hannah, Luke and Jovi settled in by the fire. Steele had wandered off to talk to some family friends. Jovi couldn't help but be bothered by the coolness she had felt when she had told him she would be staying. "Hannah, does Steele have a thing with someone?" Jovi asked quietly. She didn't really want Luke to hear her asking. She thought by the way he had acted, that she had upset him or crossed some kind of boundary enforced by someone else.

"I don't think so. He was in a relationship with his high school sweetheart for a long time. They were the on again and off again type. He hasn't done much dating that I know of since they broke up for good."

"Who did he date?" She asked. She wondered about the woman with the long stare.

"Stacey Webster. She left town. She always wanted to travel the world. Steele never did. She does something with journalism now and Instagram. Why do you ask?" Hannah winked at Jovi. "Are you interested?" She elbowed her.

"I don't know. Maybe? He doesn't seem like he is interested in me though. Anyway, I can't be dating right now. I need to focus on wrapping up in the city and closing on the orchard." Jovi said. Hannah softened.

"Jovi, I don't want to speak out of turn, but what you should be focused on is making a true home, and that may include more than just work. You obviously do that well. I know you will crush opening the orchard and put the time in, but don't forget how important people are in your life."

Jovi gave Hannah a huge hug. "I'm going to miss you so much when I go back." She wiped at tears that she could no longer keep inside.

"Don't worry. We will talk every day, and I'll be there the day you move in. Luke and I will help move your stuff in, and I'll bring dinner complete with dessert." Jovi had never had a best friend before. She could feel that Hannah meant it. She would be there in pretty life events and the ugly ones as well.

"I'm so lucky to have met you, Hannah. Thank you."

"Anytime, and I mean it. If you are having a hard time back there, call. I made the move from the city too. It's hard to go back when you finally figure out what's ahead."

When Jovi laid down that night, her head was full. All the people she had met, the friendships she had made, her weird interaction with Nick (She had forgotten to mention that to Hannah), and her possible spark with Steele. *Why had he acted so off?* It had been a day. Tomorrow was her last day in town, and she couldn't help but feel the tug of sadness in her heart. This was where she was supposed to be. She didn't want to leave.

Chapter 5

Sunday afternoon Jovi stepped into her apartment. She felt so out of place, like she had been gone much longer than a few days. She felt something had been awakened in her. This shoe no longer fit her foot. She had stopped by her future orchard before leaving, and she managed to see Hannah. Jovi was in tears again when they said goodbye. Hannah had promised she would meet her in the parking lot immediately after closing. Hannah and Luke would help her move in, and they would eat some Cozy Kitchen specials for lunch. "Promise me you will call if you need me. None of this will feel easy. The breakup with Dylan will feel rawer when you are back there. Woodsburrow really pulls at your soul." Jovi had promised she would call.

She unpacked her things, washed her clothes, and got ready for the work week. The more she went through the motions, the emptier she felt being back. How had she been living the life of a ghost all these years?

She decided there was no time like the present to do a purge and declutter. She had to do something to keep herself busy. Jovi spent the rest of the day creating an oversized load that barely fit in her Subaru to take to the local Goodwill. Most of her décor wouldn't have a place in her new home. She only kept sentimental items, a painting her mom had done of her grandparent's home, her quirky cuckoo clock she had stumbled on from her favorite shop in the city, and her quilts that her grandmother had made her. The other modern items got thrown out. Her wardrobe was next to be analyzed. She had too many outfits she had worn with Dylan and past boyfriend's to different events around the city. She wouldn't need more than a few fancy outfits in Woodsburrow. She made a note to do some shopping for more clothes that would be appropriate for working around her orchard before she left town.

When she finished, she was satisfied that everything she was bringing with her would fit in the Subaru. Her new house was coming partially furnished like her apartment had been. She was determined that she would be ready to finish her work obligations without any major headaches.

By noon the next day, all she felt was a headache. The atmosphere had become so toxic from the layoffs. Her manager pushed her harder than he ever had before. It was as if he was determined to squeeze everything out of her that he could before he didn't have that luxury anymore. Jovi began to see she had been doing her own job and his. *What did that man do all day?* He sent nasty emails nagging her on deadlines and handed her more projects to her already full plate.

She was grateful for her lunch break. She tried to drown out the noise and pulled out her phone. The first thing she was greeted with was pictures of Dylan and Izzy the intern announcing their relationship publicly. She quickly closed her phone screen and absently listened to her coworkers complain about the company and their own workloads. Her mind felt stormy.

She sent her mom a text asking when she wanted to see her for dinner and to see how she was feeling. "Hey sweetie. Sunday for lunch is a good time for us. I'm feeling fine, just tired. We had an ultrasound of the baby. It still looks like a jellybean yet, but I can show you when you come. Can't wait to hear about your trip!" Her mother was always so positive and confident. *How did she manage it?* Even when they could barely afford to keep the electricity on and had to eat the same $1 meal from McDonald's every night, she would still sing and paint and laugh with Jovi. Jovi wanted to have some of that in herself. Her mom always believed tomorrow would be a better day. Jovi needed to believe that now, or at least pretend until she genuinely believed.

When Jovi got home after work, she called Caroline Grant. She had made a list of things she could start working on prior to closing to keep her mind busy. The first thing she wanted to do, was find out how to make Lynn's famous pies. If anyone could hunt down Lynn's pie recipe, it would be Lynn's best friend Caroline. Caroline promised she would look around and let her know. She was thrilled by Jovi's interest in Lynn's history. "I'll make some calls and see what I can dig up. Hang in there, sunshine. We are so excited for your big move! You are going to love it here." Despite how terrible her day had been, Jovi's focus was shifted back to the orchard and away from this mundane life in the city.

After getting out of the shower later that evening, her phone buzzed. Jovi grabbed it and discovered a text from Dylan. "I know we ended things a little harsh, but if you ever still want to hang out, let me know."

Was this creep serious? He wanted to make her a sidepiece, his number two when number one wasn't available. Her first thought was to call Hannah. *Was that being obnoxious that she thought she had a problem that warranted a vent call on day one back home?* But Hannah had told her to call if she needed her. *Why was she overthinking this?*

Jovi dialed Hannah's number. She picked up immediately. "Happy 54 days!" Her singsong voice rang out. Jovi hesitated a beat too long. "What's wrong?" Hannah asked.

"This day was way harder than I expected. The amount of toxicity around me has me wanting to hole up in my room." Jovi confided. She told her about her manager, the atmosphere at work, and the text from Dylan. "Not to mention he announced their relationship online today. What kind of back door hookup does he think I am?"

"Absolutely not, Jovi. He has lost his mind. All that power has gone to his head. He probably disrespects all women like that. We are just a pretty thing to display like a trophy instead of a human being. This is not about you. I've got dinner plans with Luke. I'm going to call you again tomorrow and check in, okay?"

"Yeah."

"You need to block his number. Don't allow him to try to sneak back in. Nothing good will come from that." They said good night, and she settled in with some Italian and a glass of wine.

She knew Hannah was right. Dylan was a condescending jerk. The worst part? She was so lonely she considered it. She imagined showing up at his condo and convincing him she was better for him than the intern. *What would he say about her house purchase?* He would call it frivolous and useless. This man did not deserve any more of her time or thoughts, ever. She pulled her phone out and blocked him. Then she turned on *The Notebook* and turned off the lights.

Tuesday, Wednesday, and Thursday were all the same. The days went fast because Jovi buried herself in her work. Hannah and Jovi talked daily. Friday finally came, and Jovi was never more thankful the weekend was here. When she arrived home after work, she had a package waiting for her outside her front door. She brought it into her kitchen and tore it open. A letter sat on top. Caroline had not only found Lynn's apple pie recipe but her entire personal cookbook. Jovi flipped through cider recipes and apple cobbler variations. Caroline had hit pure gold. Jovi poured over the pages handwritten and filled with smudges and notes along the edges. She could see Lynn baking as if she were right next to her in real time. She read until late into the night. Lynn had such pride for her baking and strived for perfection. She felt a kindred spirit in Lynn and was so honored to take her beautiful recipes and breathe life into them again.

That weekend, Jovi spent all of her time trying any and all apple varieties she could get her hands on at the store this time of year. She knew these varieties were subpar to what would grow in her orchard, but she wanted to practice with how different varieties behaved in different recipes. She was starting with Lynn's apple crumble pie. She thought the easiest way to get a feel for her flavor and baking type was to get her hands dirty.

She had done some baking, but not much, and she certainly had never rolled out a pie crust. The crust was the biggest learning curve. Many other recipes in Lynn's book required a similar handmade crust, so it was best to practice and get the technique down now. By the sixth pie, she was finally happy enough with the result. It at least didn't look like a child had made it, and Jovi's soul felt renewed.

Sunday afternoon came, and Jovi made the drive to her mom's house with two of the pies she had decided were good enough for human consumption. Her mother greeted her in a hug at the door. "Did you bring pie? You didn't have to bring anything, Jov." She was glowing and draped in different colorful patterns with free-flowing fabrics.

"It's a part of my new adventure. I'll tell you all about it." When Jovi stepped into the house, Silas attacked her like a dinosaur.

"Roar!" He yelled.

"The most frightening dino I've ever seen!" Jovi laughed and gave Silas a huge hug and a kiss.

"Hey, sisi. Mommy is having a new baby in her tummy!"

"I heard bud. Are you excited?"

"Yeah. He can play with me all the time then."

"That sounds like fun! Are you going to share your dinosaurs with the baby?"

"No. He will have to get his own." And then he tromped off to finish his game.

"We don't know the baby's gender yet." Her mom said. "But Silas is dead set on a brother." She led them over to the dining room where David was bringing out the food he had prepared.

In the corner, the door to her mother's studio had been left open. David had added on that room for her mom when she had moved in. Giant windows covered the outside wall to let in as much light as possible. The colors on the wall were her mother's chosen combination. Chaos looked like it had erupted everywhere in there, and the afternoon sun made everything glow. Jovi knew that was exactly how her mother liked it. It made her smile.

She had been working on some beautiful charcoal drawings of people. There was a very pregnant woman, an elderly couple in an embrace, and a child with his mother. She had watercolor images in another portion. Broken pieces of charcoal and brushes drying for the next time they would stroke canvas, laid on various small tables throughout the room.

Her mom could see so much beauty in everyday things. She was so happy her art had made it big. She no longer had to work her minimum wage jobs to get by. David had a great job, and she was a successful artist. Jovi felt gratitude that her mom was able to spend her days creating beautiful pieces of magic.

David was an excellent cook, and the smells of beef stew and warm buns mixed invitingly in the air. "Jovi, it is so good to see you." They did a hug handshake greeting. It wasn't so much that their touch was awkward, and more that David knew Jovi wasn't a hugger like her mom was. "I found this classic series of books on my last trip that I thought you might like."

Jovi looked down to see 1ˢᵗ editions of *The Great Gatsby, Great Expectations*, and *A Christmas Carol.* He loved giving others gifts, and he knew how much Jovi loved reading and old items. This was truly a kind gift. "David these are beautiful. Thank you!" Whatever role David was playing in her life, he was a good one.

"Tell us all about your new adventure." He said.

They sat and ate. Jovi shared the details from the layoff to the apartment for sale. "I'm moving to Woodsburrow. I bought an orchard that I plan to expand to include a pumpkin patch. My plan is to open September 1st."

"That sounds lovely, Jovi. We would love to come see your place. I'm sure it's an absolutely charming property. That's a huge undertaking, but I know that if anyone can do it, it's you. You always have such a dedicated and hardworking personality, and you obviously have a clear vision for it."

"If you need help with any of the business finance stuff, I'm here. That's almost exclusively what I do at work. Some of the paper gets a little tricky. Don't be afraid to ask." David said.

Jovi was surprised at the lack of warnings that they had issued her and was overwhelmed by the support. "You don't think it's crazy?" She asked.

"Jovi, you haven't been happy there in the city. We haven't seen you flourish; you know bask in the sun like a cat." Her mom grinned. "You have been dating men you have no intentions on staying with, living in an apartment that doesn't match your aura and in fact looks almost identical to the sample unit it was when you moved it years ago. Starting a business is hard, moving is hard, but watching your life pass you by without getting your hands dirty and living it, is worse." David agreed.

"A property is a good investment. If something goes wrong, we can figure out a backup plan. But now is a time in your life to be taking risks and figuring out what you want. It sounds like the perfect environment for a business like that. You may surprise yourself with how well you do.

Let me know if you need other vendors or business contacts."

"I am grateful for the support, and the lack of negative judgement, you guys. You really think I've been unhappy? Hannah said it was obvious that I hate the city. I never noticed." Her mom nodded.

"You haven't been happy there. When you were younger, you had the most beautiful imagination. You used to love singing and wearing the color purple. You would pour over classic books and beg to spend most of your waking hours outside. As you got older, you got more private about all those things that made you, you. I thought it was just teenager behavior, but you never came back Jovi. You just neutralized yourself. You don't have to be the same person you were as a child, but you do have to be somebody. Be you. I don't know why you ever thought that wasn't enough. You are enough just as who you are."

Later in the kitchen while Jovi and her mom were washing dishes and Silas and David were playing in the living room, Jovi asked her mom, "Is that what raising me was like to you? Watching life move by without you?" Her mom turned to face her.

"Absolutely not, Jovi. I would do all of it again in a heartbeat. I told you, every child is a blessing. Now my oldest is a beautiful woman creating her own places of beauty in this world. I met some amazing people as a single Mom. I got to see generosity and kindness that not everyone is privy to in this messy world. I worked hard, yes, but the things I discovered about myself were important. The person I am with David would never be if not for that time. I savor all the bits of life. You have to be able to relish in the things that set your soul on fire, little or large. Pursue things that fuel that fire. Sometimes they work, and sometimes they don't. Sometimes it's easy, and sometimes it's hard. Don't be afraid to let yourself out. Don't dull yourself or live in such hesitation. You are a vibrant human being. I'm so proud of you." Her mom squeezed her tightly. Jovi knew she was right. She was the queen at making herself "less than" or smaller so she wasn't too bold.

Why did she do that? She should be herself and all of herself. If someone didn't like her for who she was, they didn't deserve a spot in her life. She almost never took chances. Jovi liked to do things that she knew would turn out fine. Her mom's energy flowed and was so relaxed. She took chances all the time without worrying about things like that. "I guess I've always felt flawed or like people see me as a victim. I don't want that label or their imperfections to be projected on me." Jovi looked down.

"I'm really sorry I could never give you that father to help balance raising you. He is a part of you that I know feels like a stranger sometimes. He didn't want the commitment of being a father. He insisted on me having an abortion. He even brought me to the clinic and gave me money for it. I had to choose you or him, I never thought once that losing you would be worth having him. You would have made his life, the way he saw it, ruined. He didn't know I didn't do it. I think that's best. He would be livid and not grateful. He is the shameful one. You are a miracle." Jovi and her mom embraced. "Follow your heart Jovi. Please keep living vibrantly."

Chapter 6

The next week of work was ticking by. Jovi spent her evenings picking out the tree varieties that she would add this year. She had settled on some HoneyGold and Honeycrisp. She figured she would need more fresh picking variations that customers would recognize. The heritage trees were known to be excellent keepers and bakers, and it sounded like Lynn had some really good fresh eating apples, but apples with names that people knew that would bring new customers who may not be familiar with the old orchard. She had also decided to open the barn as a gift shop with local artisans and her various apple bakery items. She couldn't wait to get started.

The days and weeks had crept by. She had only a few weeks left of work, and she was thankful it was Saturday. She had reprieve from that horrible stuffy office. She sat on her couch with her hot cup of coffee with creamer. She always drank it that way now. She was reading *The Great Gatsby*. It was one of her favorite books. As she read, she thought about what life might look like in her new home. She pictured the afternoon sun shining on her living room. The plush green couch with the waved back was long enough and deep enough for her to lay on while she read. She couldn't wait.

She heard a knock on her door. Jovi jumped. She had been so deep in thought she had felt the couch underneath her. Jovi set her cup down and went to the door. A knock came again. *Who was it, and why were they so impatient?* She opened the front door.

"Hello!!"

"Hannah!!!" She screamed, and they embraced. "What are you doing here?"

"I came to surprise you! I can't have you wasting away here. We are going to have a girl's day! Also, can I spend the night?"

"Of course." Jovi answered with laughter.

"Show me around!" Hannah came in and set down her bags. "I hope you have started packing already Jovi because this apartment is not you."

"I have, and I know. When I got back all I could think of was how dull everything was and comparing it to the eclectic style of the new house and how much I love the colors and the boldness."

"That's my girl!" Hannah smiled. "Jovi is awakening!" Jovi got Hannah a cup of coffee, filled up her own, and they caught up on the couch. Hannah had been doing some wedding planning, or dreaming was the better word for it. "I just have so many ideas, the more I come up with the more I don't know where to actually start."

"I'll help when I get moved in. We can sit down and start to take some actual action. Isn't that your advice for me?" Jovi said. Hannah nodded.

"You are absolutely right. I am so crippled with wanting everything to be perfect that I am afraid to start."

"Start with the date." Jovi said. "You and Luke pick a date, and we will fill in the rest. "

Hannah and Jovi headed out to go shopping. Jovi had told her she needed to still update her wardrobe, and Hannah thought that was the perfect adventure for today.

They tried on outfits at outdoor shops and farm and home stores. They went to secondhand shops to find eclectic Victorian pieces that might match her new home. They got lunch at the best Asian restaurant in town. "This is probably the only thing that isn't better in Woodsburrow." Hannah said, and they laughed. "Luke said Steele asked when you are moving in."

"He did?" Jovi asked.

"Yeah. Maybe you are wrong that he isn't interested." Hannah replied.

"Maybe." *Steele had been thinking about her?* She couldn't believe it, and the thought sent chills down her spine.

"Are you still interested?" Hannah asked.

"I don't think I've ever had this much of an immediate attraction to a man before." Jovi answered.

"So, a definite yes then." Hannah winked.

That night they drank wine, watched movies, and laughed uncontrollably. Jovi showed Hannah Lynn's cookbook. "This is the coolest Jovi!" Hannah said as she flipped through the pages. "Are you planning on featuring her recipes?" She asked. "I can help with that."

"Yes, and actually I was thinking about keeping Autumn Gold Orchard and doing a whole ode to Lynn thing. I can't help but be impressed that Lynn created this entire place from nothing."

"I love it." Hannah clapped her hands together. "I can't wait for opening day." She smiled.

Hannah left the next morning taking a few boxes of clothes that Jovi wouldn't be using in the next few weeks and treasures for her new house. Jovi was heartbroken to see her go, but her confidence in her decision had grown. Living boldly felt good.

On her last day of work, she could not have been more thrilled. She would close on her house tomorrow, and she was beyond ready. Hannah was just as excited, as evidenced from the number of celebratory pictures she had sent her this morning. She finalized all her projects and handed her current load to Sue. Her co-workers were going to the bar that evening and invited her to join. Many had not found new jobs yet, some were moving for a job, but Jovi was over it. These people had not been friends or friendly to her in all the years she worked there. She was not going to waste her last night in town listening to these people complain. She could guarantee that none of them would be excited to hear about her new adventure. So, in brand new Jovi fashion, she declined. The grayness that had swallowed everyone whole would not take Jovi. She was living in color and not going back.

Jovi hurried home and started the night with a run. She ran through her favorite parks. She watched couples strolling together in the beautiful evening air. Spring was in full swing, and summer was around the corner. The leaves were starting to grow, and the snow had officially left the shady areas. The Earth was on fire with growth, and Jovi was ready to match it with her own. Was she ready to start dating again as well? It had been months since her break up with Dylan. After her string of failures, if she were to date, she needed to be more cautious. She could not be dating men who were wildly unmatched to herself. She needed to continue evolving into the person she was and needed to ensure the person beside her would assist in that journey and not hinder it. She needed to trust her instincts.

Jovi thought about Steele. *If he was interested, was he worth taking a chance on? Did they have the right chemistry?*

Jovi packed her Subaru and ordered her favorite take out. She savored each bite as she read. Tomorrow was the day she would become a small business owner and a homeowner. She couldn't wait.

***

After closing, she walked out of the downtown office in Woodsburrow with a chain of keys to Hannah and Luke cheering. *Was that balloons?* She felt a huge sigh of relief. Leaving the city had felt like shedding a bad layer of skin. They celebrated in the middle of the street and Jovi knew she had never been happier.

They spent the rest of the day cleaning the new house and moving furniture and boxes into their rightful rooms. They had stopped for delicious burgers and fries. They lounged on the porch and gorged themselves on Hannah's prized macrons. They were strawberry and pistachio and almost too beautiful to eat.

Afterwards, Jovi and Hannah passed each other photos that they had found in one of the side tables while moving in. They examined them closely. "That is definitely Lynn." Luke remarked while he looked over Hannah's shoulder. "These are incredibly old though. This looks like when she first bought the place." Lynn was vibrant and hopeful. There were pictures of her laughing on her porch with friends. Another picture she was planting the first trees in the orchard.

"Is that a man with her?" Hannah asked.

"I thought she never married." Jovi said.

"That doesn't mean she was never in love though. Look at the way she is lit up with him there, and he is planting trees with her. If that doesn't show commitment, I don't know what does." Jovi nodded.

"A mystery."

There was another picture someone had taken a picture of Lynn baking in her kitchen. Jovi thought the kitchen looked almost identical to this day. Her pies sat one by one on the counter, waiting for their turn in her double oven. Jovi loved the photo and hoped she could keep up with Lynn's tenacity. She planned on framing a few of them.

Hannah and Luke left around suppertime. Jovi was at peace. She made a simple dinner of tomato soup and grilled cheese and ate it at the formal dining table she had inherited with the house. The wood on the table was aged and intricate details lined the legs. She ran her hands along the details and the scars it held. It was full of its own history she would never know. She listened to the spring peepers singing as the sun was starting to set.

After her quiet dinner, she played The Beetles and started filling her massive bookshelves with her book collection. She took the three that David had given her and set them towards the middle. She smiled. It was such a simple touch that made those shelves seem like they were built to be hers. She lost herself in the music and her books.

Chapter 7

She was startled by the sound of truck tires pulling into the driveway. Jovi was reminded that she was all alone in the middle of nowhere. She hadn't locked the door and had no form of protection to keep herself safe. Through her heart beating fast in her chest and her hands shaking, she turned on the switch to the porch light and peaked out the front window. She relaxed almost immediately. She knew exactly who it was. The man got out of the truck and walked to the front door. He looked uneasy. *Was he talking to himself?* Jovi watched Steele run his hand through his hair three times from the truck to her front door.

Jovi open the door before he could knock. "Hi, Steele. It's nice to see you. What brings you by?" Jovi asked.

"I'm sorry I didn't call first. I don't have your number. I don't want to be rude or assuming in coming over here. Everyone was saying around town that you were moving in today. I know you have a lot on your plate, but I've been sitting here kicking myself for not saying anything when I last saw you. I don't even know if you are seeing someone, but I'd really like to get your number and take you out sometime." Jovi turned red.

"You do?"

"You don't?" He asked searching her face for the answer. "I haven't done much dating so I am not sure I am doing this right or reading the signs correctly, but I can't stop thinking about you. I wasn't willing to just wait to bump into you again." Jovi's heart was beating a million miles a minute.

"The last time I saw you, you didn't even say goodbye. You just got weird and walked away. I was really enjoying our time together, a lot." She confided.

"I was enjoying our time too. I haven't dated since breaking up with Stacey. She always just was around. I've never pursued a woman before. I have absolutely no skills with this at all. I hadn't even thought about dating when you showed up. Then you said you were staying, and I couldn't believe what I was hearing."

"I wasn't ready either, but you are hard to ignore." Jovi answered. "I'd love to go out some time."

Steele grabbed her phone before she had a chance to change her mind and put in his number. He slipped it back into her hand and paused. He cradled her fingers like they were fragile. He leaned in and kissed her cheek. He didn't linger. He wasn't looking for more. It felt like a thank you kiss, and it made her head feel fuzzy. "Call me. I'm free Friday. Maybe you would be willing to show me the orchard sometime? What are you calling it?"

"I'm keeping the name the same as Lynn's, Autumn Gold Orchard."

"Keeping with tradition, huh? You are going to find yourself acclimating with the locals fast." Steele said.

"I hope so. I'd love for them to get as excited about Autumn Gold as I am."

"Well, you have me won over." He smiled. She felt like she was floating.

Where did this man come from? He made her feel like he was totally invested in every word she said. He listened intently and wanted her to pursue her dreams and succeed. *Oh man would I like to see that beautiful man naked.* She promised she would call, and Steele drove down the road. She felt the warmth he had left with her even as she went inside and locked the door.

The next day, Charlie and Caroline arrived early. Caroline pulled Jovi into the largest vice grip of a hug and turned to start bringing out the gifts she had brought. "You didn't have to do this Caroline." Jovi said. "Charlie and you coming today is more than what I could ask for."

"I know dear, but this is what neighbors are for." Caroline answered. She had canned pie fillings, handmade cheeses, asparagus, and fresh milled flours. Charlie unloaded his toolbox and headed for her tractor. Caroline grabbed the buckets and shovels from the truck bed and went to fill up the buckets with water. "Let Charlie give you your lesson, and then we will get these trees in the ground." She said.

Jovi followed Charlie into the orchard barn where the tractor had been parked. Charlie examined the tractor. "Actually, Lynn did a surprisingly good job in maintaining her." He remarked. "She is old, but she looks the same as when she bought her. I'm going to change out some spark plugs for you and fill up the gas tank. I probably should check the oil as well. Then I can show you how to drive it."

Jovi watched as Charlie tinkered with her tractor. He was so methodical and so steady handed she couldn't believe it. "You are very good at this." She observed.

"I love machinery, especially old machinery." Charlie replied. "I drag Caroline to auctions and buy all the old machinery we can find. We take it home, I fix it up, and then we sell it. It's my hobby."

"Wow," was all Jovi could manage. He looked like he could have done the tune up blindfolded.

Charlie showed Jovi the gas and the break and how to drive the tractor. They were both a bit shocked however, when the tractor started up the first try. Jovi showed Charlie where she would be planting her pumpkin patch and asked if he could do the garden as well. He nodded and shooed her along to catch back up with Caroline.

Caroline and Jovi grabbed the buckets, shovels, and mulch. They carried them in the back of the orchard where they would add the additional row of trees. Caroline walked her through the proper sizing of the hole as the first little tree soaked in a bucket. Jovi held the tree straight as Caroline demonstrated how to properly fill and pack the hole. It needed to be stiff enough to hold the tree upright but not so much that it compacted the roots. They followed it with mulch. "Congratulations. You have planted a tree!"

"Amazing. I can't believe this sad little twig will grow into a mighty tree with apples everywhere. It's crazy to imagine."

"Transformations are incredible. It's some of the best parts of farming and the biggest mysteries in life. There are periods of growth and of rest and both contribute to the revolution that takes place within." Caroline smiled. She glanced over at where Charlie was plowing. They seemed to always be in tune to where each other was. They orbited each other.

"How did you meet Charlie?" Jovi asked. "It's amazing to watch you two work together, and you spend so time much doing it. I can't believe you don't get sick of each other."

"I met Charlie when I was very young and working at the ice cream shop in town. Charlie would drive his precious truck to the shop every Monday and Friday night, when he knew I would be working, and bought the same vanilla and chocolate cone with three scoops. He came in for months and we chatted every time about the same subjects before he asked me out on a date. We spent hours talking and laughing. We never looked back. Charlie is my best friend. There is no on in the world I'd rather spend time with, shoveling barns, picking beans in the heat of the summer, or a romantic dinner made by someone else. It doesn't matter. Time with him is time well spent."

"People always say you know. Up to this point, I've never had that thought, that certainty." Jovi said.

"Then those men definitely weren't the ones. You do know. It's important to listen and act when you feel it though. Having a partner, a true partner, isn't something people should miss out on. It adds spice to life and forces you to grow in ways you otherwise wouldn't." Caroline rubbed Jovi's arm. "Keep vigilant. He could be closer than you think." She winked.

The two worked until noon chatting about the town's history and different people Jovi was likely to run into or may need for help. Jovi asked questions about Lynn and what she was like, and she was more than willing to share all the stories she could remember. Apparently, Lynn had been quite fierce. Whether she was dealing with droughts, or teenage property destruction, she handled it with grace and a smile. But, when noon arrived, the entire day's work was complete. The Grants were the most efficient people Jovi thought she had ever met.

They ate sandwiches on the front lawn. Jovi had not been that hungry in a long time. It felt good to spend the day physically moving her body outside instead of being stuck at a desk. "Jovi, I think you are a very capable human, and most of the stuff you need for this place will come. We live in a very safe community but having some way of protecting yourself is something you shouldn't wait to get. Police response time would be well over 20 minutes here. It's not just people either, you have wildlife on and surrounding your property that could do some damage. Just prioritize that as you are getting settled." Charlie smiled.

"I actually had the same thought last night when Steele came over and surprised me." Caroline's head popped up fast, and she raised her eyebrows at Jovi.

"Did he?"

"Yeah, he did. He asked me to go out some time." "Did you say yes?"

"I think so." Jovi replied. "He seemed very nervous. It was all hard to process."

"Well clarify that. That's a perfect place to start." Caroline winked at Jovi. "He is a man with a generous heart who loves his family fiercely and serves the community often. I couldn't think of a better match for you."

"Caroline, don't scare her off before they have even gone out." Charlie looked at Caroline sternly.

"I'm just giving background. We are happy to see you taking some chances and settling in." She said. "Charlie is right about having some protection though. It isn't often we need ours, but we are thankful to have it when we do. We adore you dear and can't wait to see you bloom."

Since the Grants left before the afternoon had hardly began, Jovi had plenty of daylight left. She was so relieved not to be spending any more of her days wasting life in an office. She went into the house and made herself a cup of tea. She sat in her living room with the afternoon sunlight pouring over her and her green couch. She wrapped her grandmother's quilt around her. *Just like I imagined it.* She thought with a smile.

She considered her options for some protection. She didn't feel comfortable buying a gun. She thought she should some probably learn some gun safety and usage skills before owning a firearm. So, what could she do that felt safer and was quicker to obtain? Jovi set her teacup in the sink and headed upstairs to shower.

She had a list of things to pick up in town, so she started at the top. The grocery store to pick up groceries, since she hadn't had the time since moving in, Drury Lane to see Hannah. Jovi picked up some of her lemon cookies and more sourdough bread while she was chatting. She mailed her mom a letter from her new address, and then she headed to the hardware store. Although her property had come with quite a few tools and machines, there were still garden tools that she would need. Tools that required sharp edges to work had rusted. She grabbed a rake, trowels of different sizes, a wheelbarrow, and pruning shears. They had a large selection of seeds, so she pursued that as well.

As she shopped throughout what seemed like the entire store, Jovi ended up in the paint aisle looking at colors that would go in the orchard barn, she kept glancing around looking for Steele. She wanted to directly accept his invitation. All that nervousness had confused her. *Had she accepted?* She couldn't remember. She really liked Steele and wanted to do this dating thing the right way.

She had dated so many losers who were losers from the start, but Steele was different. Jovi actually felt the chemistry, the heat between them. Steele was generous and patient. The losers she had dated before were demanding and cared too much about their appearance and not enough about the world around them. She had found them handsome but had never been overwhelmed by the sensations that they had made her body feel. She had felt indifferent. Well, she wasn't feeling indifferent today. She wanted Steele to see her as differently as she was seeing him. She wanted him to see the real her and know she was independent, assertive, and enjoyed her quiet space. Jovi wanted to be seen as a whole piece, undulled. While she was mustering up her courage, she couldn't believe it when Nick rounded the corner.

Chapter 8

"You've got to be kidding me!" Jovi mumbled. *What is he doing here?* Nick did not remind Jovi of a man that had much need for hardware.

"Jovi! You are looking radiant today. I'm so glad you are all moved in. I can take you out and show you everything in our town now." He winked at her.

Why was this man leaning in so close again? He brushed his words against her ear, and Jovi pulled herself back. She felt extremely uncomfortable every time this man was around. It was time to listen to those instincts. "Nick, I don't want to go out with you." Jovi stated with force. She looked up and saw Steele walking away. *Did he think she was interested in someone else? In this guy?*

"I think that's a mistake. You and I would be great together. Successful realtor, small business owner, not to mention we would be the most attractive couple in town." This man was exactly like the kind of men she had dated in the city. They were overconfident in themselves, and every action they took was for personal gain. She was not having this man follow her anymore.

"Nick, I am not interested, and you need to back off." Jovi stated more assertively this time.

"Is there a problem, Jovi?"

It was Luke! Jovi looked over her shoulder to see him in uniform.

"I was just welcoming Jovi to the town. It's so nice to have fresh faces around." He slipped his arm over her shoulder and grinned at Luke. Jovi shoved Nick off her and took a step towards Luke. Luke stepped toward Nick and placed his body between Jovi's and Nick's.

"It looks like your welcome, isn't. Leave Jovi alone, or I'll assist her in filing a complaint."

Nick shook his head and walked away. He called over his shoulder, "A mountain out of a molehill, sir. I'm leaving now."

"Thanks Luke." Jovi was rattled. She didn't think Nick would have walked away without Luke intervening.

"Has he been bothering you repeatedly, Jovi?"

"He did before the Firelight Festival, and I told him to buzz off. He obviously didn't understand the word no."

"He didn't today either. I've had a problem with complaints of woman being harassed. He's had some rape charges filed, but they never stick. His family has some ties to the best attorneys in this town. That makes him more dangerous. I take those recurring filings seriously. Be careful and call me immediately if you have another run in with him." Luke handed her his business card. He studied her face.

"Do you want to sit down Jovi? You look shaken up. Not that I blame you. I just want you to be safe." Jovi shook her head.

"I just want to leave now. Sorry." Jovi took her cart to the register to check out. Steele hadn't even said hello. He thought she was interested in Nick. *How could she have messed this up before it had even begun?* Thank goodness Luke had showed up when he did. *Who knows what Nick would have done to make her submit to his requests?*

Her eyes blurred with tears as she loaded her Subaru. She needed to focus on herself just like she had planned. *Who needed a man anyway?* Lynn had never had one and seemed to have lived a good life. Maybe they were too strong of women to have someone else around all the time. She started her car and drove away.

Jovi pulled into the Humane Society parking lot. She needed a dog. A companion, and protector of herself and her home. It was where she would start until she could get some gun safety training. She could use some consistent company as well. She loved her quiet time, but the orchard could get lonely if she spent extended time there without people around. She had always wanted a dog. She remembered writing letters to Santa as a child asking only for a puppy. The apartment her mom had rented didn't allow dogs, so that puppy never came. In the city, her complex had been the same, and anyway she had never had enough time to dedicate to having one. She had stopped for dog food, a leash, and some bowls. The store had a small toy section, she had found some balls and various chew toys. To say she was excited was an understatement. She headed in hoping her dog was just beyond the doors.

Although the kennel was not overwhelmed with dogs, it was heartbreaking to see the amount that was there waiting to find homes. Jovi wandered around looking at every one of them. They had ridiculously small toy breed dogs, huskies, a few labs, and some who's breeds were completely non-identifiable. Some were loud and others quiet. She rounded the corner dog of kennels and saw a medium sized dog with long hair with a beautiful black and white pattern. She wagged her tail as Jovi approached, and the long hair on her tail swayed. Jovi asked the attendant to see the elegant dog and took her for a walk out back. The dog was thrilled to be outside. She licked Jovi over and over again. There was a fenced in area that she was allowed to run in. Jovi removed her leash, and she ran in circles like she had never ran before. "Zoomies!" the attendant called it. She returned to Jovi for some affection and happily played ball with her. Jovi knew they had bonded, and she would take her home.

"Would you like to see any of the other dogs?" The attendant asked.

"No." Jovi replied. "She's the one."

Duchess jumped onto the front seat of the car like she knew that was where she should ride. Duchess was one of the heirloom varieties that grew in her orchard, and the royalty of it fit the dog perfectly. Duchess was a youthful dog. The attendant had said she was only a year old. They knew she was a setter. Her family had brought her to the shelter because they were moving and couldn't take her with. She was friendly with children and tended to bark when people entered the kennel. That was fine with Jovi, she wanted Duchess to tell her if someone was on her property.

Jovi let Duchess walk around and get comfortable with the house. The kennel had said that it might take her a few weeks to get comfortable in a new home. They told her to expect some signs of stress and to give her time to settle in. It wasn't long after unloading the groceries that Duchess had abandoned her sniffing of her new home, and was curled up on the green coach, sleeping.

Jovi turned on some Frank Sinatra and let the feelings of her home permeate the place. She worked methodically and sang to the music. Duchess came in and laid right at her feet. Regardless of whatever her man problem was, it had been a good day. Her newest best friend had entered her life. She was home.

Friday came, and Duchess went with Jovi for their first run together. It was time to develop a sort of routine around all the newness the two of them had experienced this week. Jovi worried that Duchess wouldn't be able to keep up the entire distance, but that wasn't a problem at all. Duchess was a setter so running was as natural as breathing to her. They ended the run with breakfast and Jovi took a shower. They headed back outside to work on planting the pumpkin patch. Jovi had bought three different types of seeds for this year. She wanted to see how popular the pumpkin patch would be before she invested more time into it. She had a chosen a fairly large variety, a medium sized jack-o-lantern style and a white one to give some contrast. She planted while Duchess explored but stayed close to Jovi. Duchess began to bark when a vehicle pulled into the driveway. Jovi looked up and realized it was Steele. She met him in the driveway with Duchess close at her heels.

"I came to apologize." Steele said as he climbed out of his truck and shut his door. Duchess backed up cautiously. "Hello." He said and got down into a squatting position. He gave Duchess enough space, held out his hand and waited.

"Why do you need to apologize?" Jovi asked. "It's ok, Duchess." She scratched Duchess behind the ears and made sure her body language conveyed that Steele was not a threat. Duchess crept forward cautiously and sniffed at Steele's hand. Steele remained still. He waited for Duchess to convey she thought that he was friend and not foe.

"I let my own jealously cloud my head. I couldn't stand seeing you with another man, and I just walked away. Luke stopped in to let me know what was going on. I don't want you to think I'm the kind of man who wouldn't protect you or defend you if you needed. You aren't helpless by any means, but I'd stand by you or in front of you if the situation called. I just didn't know where we stood. Nick was standing so close to you. I didn't realize you were uncomfortable. I looked for you immediately after talking to Luke, but you were already gone. He seemed pretty concerned with how Nick had been bothering you."

Jovi grabbed Steele's hands, and Duchess began to wag her tail. They felt worn like a favorite pair of boots. Again, Jovi felt warmth that spread down to her toes. "We stand at it is currently Friday, and I'm promised a first date. Would you like a tour? I'm not dressed up for going out anywhere." She gestured at her property and looked down at her clothes.

Duchess had decided that Steele was her new favorite person. She had melted into a puddle and was letting Steele scratch her belly. "She is a beauty." Steele said. Although Jovi wasn't sure he was talking about the dog.

"She is smart too. I can't believe how well she adjusted already. She seems to love it outside."

"She was clearly made to be an orchard dog." Steele smiled. "I brought you something." He walked over to the tailgate of his truck and pulled out a giant chunk of metal.

The metal chunk was a huge apple surrounded by mighty trees. The words read "Autumn Gold Orchard" in the center. "Did you make this?" She asked. He nodded.

"Do you like it?"

"Steele this is incredible. You made me a sign! Can we hang it up today? I know just the spot." Heat rose into his face.

"I learned to do some metal work to add to the business. It gives me some other customers and uniqueness that my father didn't have. I didn't know if you would like the design or not. I've never done one without consulting with the business owner first."

"It's perfect. I love it." Jovi wrapped her arms around Steele's tall and broad body. He felt warm against her. She could hear her beating heart against his chest. They seemed to melt into each other. She pulled him away before their bodies somehow stuck.

Jovi and Steele walked straight back to the orchard barn. She grabbed a hammer, and some nails and Steele grabbed the ladder. Steele climbed up and after some adjustments to get it straight, hung the sign. The Autumn Gold Orchard logo faced the road. You could see it from the driveway. If you looked directly to the right, you could see the rows of apple trees awakening. Jovi snapped a photo. She wanted to add it to her business website.

After the sign was hung, Jovi continued the tour. They went inside the barn, and Jovi talked about the shelves she wanted to install for the artisan goods she planned on displaying. Steele listened as she detailed her vision. She had started to stack the wooden harvest crates she had been lucky to inherit on one side. The other, she had planned on updating the check-out cubical that would double as the miniature bakery. Jovi talked about how much learning Lynn's history had inspired her. "I can't believe she built this place by herself. It's impressive. I even started learning to bake with her recipes. She was such an inspirational lady. I wish I would have known her while she was alive. I plan on adding a memory wall her in her honor."

"She was a tough lady. She was kind as well. She hosted field trips for the local children. I remember coming as a child, and she made it something everyone looked forward to."

They walked together to the pumpkin patch. Jovi had all but two rows planted. Steele just grabbed a trowel and started putting seeds into the ground with her. Jovi was surprised that he was willing to just jump in, so she just went with it. They finished the patch in 15 minutes. "Thank you." She said to him. "I don't expect you to do my work for me."

"I know." He replied. "And you would never ask. But I like getting my hands dirty, and hearing you talk about this place is the most beautiful thing I've ever seen. It's a bit infectious." He smiled.

"You haven't even seen my trees yet!" Jovi said.

Jovi steered Steele over to the orchard. "Wow. Isn't it incredible how strong they look?" Jovi nodded.

"They are in really good shape. I'm expecting some good yields if the weather cooperates. Then this fall, I'll give them a good mulch. Following that up with a winter pruning, and we will really see what they can do next year. I can't wait to watch them year after year." She smiled. Steele was looking around, just as enchanted by them as she was.

Jovi went inside to grab her property map that she had been given at closing. There were areas that even Jovi hadn't seen yet. Steele was more than willing to continue their date as they wandered around her acreage. Jovi hadn't had time to do that yet, and it proved to be magical. They found a stream that was full and rushing from the spring thaw. Steele came alive when they approached the water, and Jovi watched him looking for different fish. She knew he would want to fish it; he was just too polite to ask, yet. The woods were so peaceful, and on the way back to the house, Jovi and Steele walked through them in silence, both listening to the sounds around them. They circled back into the yard. That hike had given Jovi an idea for a hayride route, and she made a mental note to draw it out so she could work on clearing a path.

"So," Steele said. "Have you spoken to any artisans yet?" She shook her head no. "We should go to the farmers' market next Sunday. It's the first one of the season. You should be able to see all the best artists, and you can talk to them all in one shot. And then we can go for ice cream after."

"I love that idea. Yes!" Jovi answered.

"I'd really like to stay longer today, but my parents are expecting me for dinner. I had a great time today. Your slice of heaven is quite the piece of gold. Duchess, I'll see you soon girl." Duchess gave into her goodbye scratches and arched her back to get a better angle.

"I had a good time too. Thank you for everything. I promise I won't be looking for free labor every time we are together though." Jovi laughed.

"I know." Steele replied. "My sister tells me acts of service is my love language. Apparently, that's why I spend so much of my time helping my dad." He smiled. "Do you know yours?"

"My what?" Jovi asked.

"Love language. My sister says it's important to speak the same language." He shrugged. "The things you learn when you have a sister." Jovi laughed.

"I don't think I've ever been asked that before. I'll have to do some research and get back to you."

"In the meantime," Steele said. "I should probably try another method just in case." Steele pulled Jovi close and tenderly, but firmly kissed her. Jovi could feel herself melting again as she leaned in. Steele carefully separated their bodies. "Good night Jovi." He said softly. He bent down to ruffle Duchess' head one last time, and he left. Jovi's head whirled. That man made her feel things she wasn't sure she could define and certainly had never felt before.

Chapter 9

"You what?!" Hannah yelled into the phone.

"We kissed." Jovi repeated.

"How come I didn't know you two were dating? This is exactly best friend material."

"I didn't even know." Jovi answered. "He asked me out, but then I thought I had screwed it up with that Nick incident."

"Luke told me about that. He gives me the heebie jeebies." Hannah shuttered through the phone. "Keep your distance from him. He tends to have tunnel vision when he wants something."

"Good to know." Jovi replied. "I've been trying to avoid him so far, and he keeps showing up. Oh, I got a dog too, Duchess."

"A dog? Do I need to invite myself up there every couple of days, so you don't forget to tell me stuff? I love dogs. I can't wait to meet her. Bring Duchess to the bakery so we can snuggle. So, Steele, are you seeing him again?"

"He invited me to go to the farmers' market on Sunday."

"OOOHH a town event! That is a big deal! I do a booth. Walk him over so I can ogle you guys. I'm so excited for you. What a perfect match!"

"I'm a little nervous it's too good to be true."

"Jovi, you deserve what is happening. You were stuck in the city. Your life is just catching up to level the score for you. Doesn't it feel good to actually live?"

***

Jovi spent the next week fixing up her barn space and tending her gardens. She learned how to hang shelves and muddled through getting them exactly right. She completely repainted her cashier area and bakery. She had ordered frames for the photographs they had found when moving in and hoped she could find other items to hang with it on the wall by the bakery. She stacked the rest of the harvest baskets, bleached buckets and cleaned so much dirt and dust. Jovi had contacted the paper to run a story about her opening the orchard on September first. She had paid for advertisements that would run the fourth of July through the end of the season, so she hoped they would be willing to run one article.

As she waited for a response, she continued to rummage through the boxes that Lynn had left behind. She had found her pie pans and different baking sheets that she cleaned up until they shined as bright as new. She would use them for baking this fall. The ones that were in poor shape, she sat on one of her shelves in the orchard barn. It gave it some character and made her feel closer to Lynn and hoped it would give her strength or luck, maybe both. She found some old cider equipment which she moved into the barn. She wasn't sure if it was in good enough shape to use, but even if it wasn't, it would look beautiful on her shelves.

Jovi had finally received an email from Matt who she had managed to convince at the paper in town that her orchard reopening was worth a story piece. She prepared for the meeting by combing through the few photographs she had found and took some new ones of her own. She had taken a few good pictures of the orchard in all its spring glory and had chosen the picture of Lynn hand planting the trees as new babies with the man working beside her and a huge smile spread across her face.

Jovi went into town for her meeting with Matt, who probably was the only employee at the paper. The meeting was brief, but Matt had asked questions about how the orchard was coming along and how she came to buy it. They talked about Lynn's legacy and that she had decided to keep the name Autumn Gold Orchard. She told him about the opening day event they would be having, and that more information would follow in her Fourth of July ad. She left Matt with the old photo of Lynn and the new photos she had taken with the trees in bloom.

After her meeting, Jovi brought Duchess over to meet Hannah. Duchess had no hesitation when she met her and smothered her with kisses almost immediately. It helped that she had made an entire batch of peanut butter bacon cookies for Duchess. "Duchess you are quite the little queen!" Hannah exclaimed. It was safe to say Duchess would love her for life.

Towards the end of the week, Hannah noticed some odd occurrences. She thought maybe she had been working too hard and chalked it up to exhaustion. She had been doing a lot more physical work than she was used to at her desk life in the city. When her head hit the pillow at night, she drifted to sleep immediately. Strangely, Duchess had begun to bark during the night at around the same time. Each night it happened, Duchess and Jovi went outside to check out what the commotion was about, and they never found anything. Jovi assumed the deer were getting close to the house to look for food. She was watching the pumpkin patch to make sure they hadn't started eating the little plants. So, it was possible her brain was just as exhausted as well.

The first odd thing was the barn appeared to have been left open the night before. Jovi always closed the barn at night because she didn't want to have racoons get inside. Jovi couldn't remember closing it, though she had assumed that she had. The next day, all four tractor tires appeared flat. She had been unable to inflate them and made a note to have Charlie come over and fix them before she had to use it next. It was possible the tires were just old and needed to be replaced. Or had they started to go flat after Charlie had ran it? Again, she wasn't sure. She hadn't been checking on it daily. On Saturday, a package that was scheduled to be delivered, never showed. After contacting the post office who told her package had been delivered, and her informing them it was in fact not at her house, the company had agreed to reship the item. At face value, any of these things could mean absolutely nothing. Jovi left the week telling herself she would take it a bit easier next week, and that she had stepped into a string of bad luck. It was better to have that now than closer to opening day.

On Sunday morning, Steele showed up at exactly nine in the morning. He was dressed in a dark green flannel shirt that made his eyes a more radiant green and blue jeans that hugged his strong legs like they were made for him. Jovi realized she was looking at him too much like a piece of

Hannah's Tiramisu and shook her head to refocus herself. She had to calm down. She wanted to concentrate on the getting to know him part today. Jovi would also be meeting vendors she hoped to display in her barn. *Focus Jovi.*

Jovi had on a bright sundress. The breeze made the fabric feel light against her skin. It was finally starting to feel like summer. The warm days had been stringing together and the cold nights had gone away.

"Are you ready to go?" Steele asked as he handed her a warm cup of coffee. Jovi moaned.

"My love language might be coffee." She smiled.

"I had them put cream and sugar in it. I wasn't sure how you normally drink it, but that's how I like mine."

"Definitely yes to cream and sugar, or flavored creamer. Something to give the coffee an extra level of something. It is just like how peanut butter needs jelly. Let me run in and get Duchess settled. It's her first time alone."

"I'd love to bring her with, but they don't allow dogs at the market, and I think it's too hot today for her to sit in my truck. She is such a good girl. You got lucky."

"I know." Jovi said as she hurried inside. *You don't know how lucky I feel.* She thought.

Jovi settled Duchess in on the couch, her favorite spot. Her blanket was spread out there for her. Jovi got her a bone and checked her water. "Be a good girl. I'll be back." Duchess wagged her tail in response. Jovi felt guilty already about leaving her alone.

Jovi and Steele talked about their families on the way to the farmers' market. Steele's brother Christopher was an investment banker in the city. Steele told her about his sister, Emma who was married and had his only nephew that was two. "He is full of personality now and my little buddy."

"My brother Silas is three. I know that's strange." Jovi wrung her hands together, clearly uncomfortable. Steele took his steady hand and placed it on top of hers.

"It's not strange. It just means your mother is youthful. That's nothing to be ashamed of." Steele spoke gently. "My parents were very young when they got married. They were in love and pregnant with my brother. They were barely 18. My dad worked his way from a shelf stocker to owner of the store. He was a great boss because of it. Never be ashamed of the things that built you."

Jovi took a deep breath. She hadn't shared her family details with anyone since leaving high school. "My mom was 16 when she had me. She never told me who my father is. She's always said he was wildly pushy about her getting an abortion, but she couldn't do it. He never knew I was born. She raised me as a single parent. She worked hard to make sure we had all the things we needed to survive. I spent a lot of time with my grandparents when she worked. They passed away five years ago, and I miss them terribly. My mom is married now to a great guy. David treats her how she always should have been treated. They are pregnant with their second child. Silas is insistent it's a brother, but they don't know what it is yet."

"I bet it's hard to not know a piece of you like that, but don't make that foolish man's loss your badge to wear. You are an incredibly strong and independent woman grown from another strong woman. You don't need anything else from that man but your life."

Jovi squeezed his hand in return. She felt like she could just be around this man. She could show him herself without muting or filter herself down, and she knew he would like her the same. It was an amazing feeling and a frightening one. She didn't even like all the pieces of herself. How could someone else?

When they arrived at the farmers' market, Jovi was impressed with the turnout. The fairgrounds had been transformed with the popup tents that were lined up in three long rows. There were enough vendors to keep the customers busy for a good hour. Jovi was impressed a town this size could put on a farmers' market that was larger than the one in the city. A folk band was set up on the amphitheater stage with a large sitting area in front. Food trucks lined both sides of the amphitheater to service that crowd. Steele held her hand as they walked vendor to vendor. They laughed and examined the booths together.

Jovi chatted with the artisans as they wandered. She saw people taking second glances all around them. She heard the whispers of people as they walked by. Jovi knew that this was the definition of going public in this town. At the end of the day, everyone would have told everyone else that Jovi and Steele were together.

As they were rounding the row and about to visit Hannah's set up, a woman approached Jovi. Steele had been chatting with a regular of his and didn't notice her corner Jovi. She squared herself with Jovi and spoke. "You should just leave well enough alone. You have no business digging up old graves and inserting yourself where you don't belong. I would think twice about your choices if I were you." Before Jovi could even register the words, she was speaking, she disappeared into the crowd.

Jovi felt the world rushing past her. What did that woman want? Who was she? She looked around but didn't see her anywhere. As she looked behind her, Steele was still completely engrossed in his conversation. She looked to Hannah's booth. She had a long line of customers waiting to purchase goods and hadn't seen Jovi getting close. No one had seen. Jovi didn't recognize the woman, but she was certainly angry with her. *How could someone she didn't know hate her that much? Why?* Jovi waited for Steele to finish his conversation as Hannah's line of customers shrank. "Ready?" Steele asked. Jovi shook her head yes.

Hannah's smile widened when she saw them coming. "Jovi! I love that dress on you! Is that one we picked up together?"

"Yes." Jovi looked down to check the dress as she said that. *That reflex was odd.* She thought. She knew what she was wearing, and what it looked like.

"It just flows on you! You look like a vision." They smiled. "And Steele, you always look ruggedly handsome. You guys are the cutest! Did you get any vendors to say yes to your orchard barn collection?" Hannah asked.

"Actually quite a few!" Jovi said. "I think I'll have plenty of takers just today, which is a huge check off on my list."

"They would be silly to say no to another opportunity to show off their wares. I'm so glad they were willing." She smiled. In true tradition, Jovi could not visit Hannah and leave without something, so Hannah slipped them some savory muffins to munch on.

After Hannah's booth, the rest of the row contained farm vendors. There were booths of fresh cut flowers, and Steele had picked out a bouquet for Jovi. "For your kitchen while you are working on those apple pies." Jovi smiled. His attention to detail when she spoke to him, was one of his characteristics that she liked best. They passed some farm booths that had freshly picked fruits and vegetables. Because it was spring, there wasn't a lot growing yet. The produce offered would grow exponentially as the growing season went on. Nevertheless, beautiful bunches of rhubarb sat next to green and purple asparagus. There were bright red radish bunches next to green ones that looked like tiny watermelons when you cut them open. There were also beautiful salad greens more robust looking than the sad Iceberg lettuce in the store. Fragrant green chives and cilantro sat in bunches. The Grant arm had a booth as well, but it was being manned by one of Charlie and Caroline's daughters-in-law. Without Caroline there to introduce them, Jovi felt like a stranger and bypassed that stop. Steele waved. She waved back with a friendly smile.

With her bouquet and bags filled with her muffins, candles, wine, artisan cheese, chives, purple asparagus and fresh spinach, Jovi was shopped out. They walked down to listen to the folk band The River Runners. For a band that had not hit even a popularity level that was respectable locally yet, they were actually really good. Jovi knew they had big things in their future.

As they approached the stage, the smell from the food trucks filled Jovi's nose. "We need to get some lunch." Jovi said while she took a deep inhale.

"What are you feeling?" Steele asked. Jovi considered her options. The food trucks were parked to the side of the stage and had BBQ, pizza, Thai, tacos, wraps, burgers, and almost anything she could think of.

"I'm going to get a pulled pork sandwich with coleslaw." She didn't realize how hungry she was. Just the smell and sound of it was mouthwatering. She chose a picnic table facing the stage with Steele, who had opted for an oversized slice of mushroom, jalapeno, and pepperoni pizza. They sat and listened to the band play.

The silence between them was comfortable. Jovi didn't feel the need to fill every second with chatter and neither did he. In the past, men had accused her of being stuck up or closed off when she just wanted to quietly observe the world around her instead of filling it with pointless chatter. It was obvious Steele enjoyed that too. She looked around as they listened.

"Steele? Have you noticed everyone has been looking at us?"

"Really?" He replied. "Why?"

"Well, there is a lot of whispering happening, but from what I can tell I think it's a big scandal that we are out together." He looked around.

"When I said I haven't done much dating since Stacey, it's more like none. I haven't dated at all, at least nothing other than a onetime attempt at dinner. They aren't used to seeing me with anyone else." Jovi looked up at him.

"No one else? That feels like a lot of pressure." She said nervously.

"No. I don't want you to feel that way." He said as he reached his hand for hers. "It's been well over a year that we haven't been together. I am just too busy to look around for women to date. Not to mention I've already told you I don't have a clue how to ask someone out." She laughed. "I always knew that Stacey wasn't the one. She was very good at taking up space, all of the space. There wasn't any room left for me to have any of it. She knew she never wanted to live here. I never would leave. There was no future in any of that. When we broke up, that was it. I haven't talked to her since and have no intention to. You and I are turning a fresh page. That's true for you as well, isn't it?" Jovi nodded.

"I've dated plenty, but it's never been serious. I've never shared about my family before."

"I'd say that would be different then." Steele and Jovi smiled at each other.

"I need to use the restroom before our ice cream joy ride." Jovi said as they got up to exit the fairgrounds.

"I'll just meet you back at the truck?" Steele nodded and headed to his truck. As Jovi was leaving the bathroom and still thoroughly rubbing her hands with hand sanitizer, Nick came into focus. He was dressed in a suit, clearly here today to drum up business. "Well Jovi, we meet again."

"Nick." She said as she moved immediately towards the parking lot.

"Any second thoughts about us?" He asked.

"There is no us." Jovi replied. Nick grabbed her wrists and pulled her tight.

"Oh, there could be an us." He spoke in a gruff voice.

Jovi was afraid of what Nick might do next. They were out of sight of the parking lot, and no one was near the restroom. Fear crept in as she struggled with her hands. If she could just get in view of the parking lot, maybe she could get someone's attention. Out of nowhere, she felt a shadow behind her. The shadow said nothing, but she felt them shove Nick backwards. He let go of her wrist, and she stumbled away from him. As she turned her head, she caught a glimpse of Steele's pants. *Steele? Where had he come from?* Before Nick could speak, Steele punched him once and smashed in his nose which sent him straight to the ground. Blood began to pour down his face. Steele grabbed him by his pressed collar and lifted him to his face. "If I ever see you near Jovi again, I'll kill you." Nick ran off without looking back.

Steele turned to find Jovi. "Are you alright?" He asked. Jovi nodded.

"I think so." She examined her wrists. They were red, but she was able to move them. "How did you know I needed help?"

"You took too long." He said. "I thought maybe you had forgotten where we parked. I didn't think I'd find you like this. We need to file a complaint with Luke. You should consider a restraining order."

"Normally I would call that too dramatic, but I think that's exactly what he deserves." Jovi replied with a still shaky voice.

Chapter 10

Steele and Jovi drove down to the station. Luke was there, and they took him through what had happened. Luke took pictures, and he filed the appropriate paperwork. It was late afternoon when they finally emerged. "Do you still want to get ice cream?" Steele asked.

"No." Jovi answered. "I'm too shook up. I wouldn't be able to eat. Can you just take me home to Duchess? He nodded and spoke softly.

"Let's go." He held her hand tightly as they walked to his truck.

They rolled down the windows, and Jovi let the wind blow in her hair. It had been a good day before Nick had shown his ugly face. She tried to close her eyes and pressed her lips together tightly to keep in the emotions that were releasing inside her. She didn't want to cry, not here. When Steele parked the truck in the driveway, Jovi grabbed her bags and headed for her house. Steele grabbed the few she couldn't carry and followed her in. Duchess was thrilled to see them, and Jovi wrapped her arms around her. Steele took her bags into the kitchen and found a vase for the flowers he had gotten. He came back into the living to see Jovi sobbing on the ground. Duchess laid in her lap like a permanent fixture. Steele sat down next to her and put his arm around her shoulder. They sat there in silence until Jovi ran out of tears. Jovi leaned her head into Steele. "I'm sorry, Jovi. He is a creep who doesn't know how to treat women with respect. I won't let him touch you again. Neither will Luke." Jovi nodded.

"I've dated some real losers, but I've never had to deal with someone like him before. The word no is more like a challenge than a refusal." Jovi stared forward. "I don't like how helpless he made me feel." Steele nodded.

"Do you want me to stay for a little while?"

"I would really like that." Jovi said looking at Steele.

Jovi put on Forest Gump and made popcorn. Steele, Jovi, and Duchess curled up on the soft green couch under her grandmother's quilt the rest of the afternoon. By the time Forest Gump was finished, Jovi was feeling better. "Thank you for staying."

"Anytime." He answered. "You can always ask me for anything, Jovi." He added. "Don't be afraid to call if anything else comes up. I'm hopeful he learned his lesson, but I'm not naive. He hasn't learned it so far. I know you pride yourself on being independent, but I am always willing to help. Everyone needs a little help sometimes."

He gently placed a kiss on Jovi's lips, and as he did, he was intentional about not guiding her with his hands. Jovi noticed he was trying not to spook her after Nick had been so aggressive. She felt the safety of his touch and the warmth he caused spread to her head. He whispered to her. "Goodnight beautiful." Then he left.

Jovi and Duchess re-entered the house, and Jovi turned the lock. She immediately walked to the back door and did the same. Duchess and Jovi went into the kitchen to make dinner. Jovi drank a glass of wine from a bottle she had bought earlier that day and listened to an oldies station. After dinner, she had a bubble bath, and by the time she had crawled into bed, she felt like she could sleep. Although Nick had been aggressive, and she had repeated interactions with him, he had never bothered her at her home. She was in a safe space. Duchess would alert her if something was wrong. She drifted off to a restless sleep.

Over the next week, Duchess and Jovi started their routine as usual. They did their daily run. Jovi showered, and they had breakfast. They went outside to do some work. Now that Jovi had specific vendors in mind with specific products, she knew what she wanted the barn to look like. She rearranged until she was satisfied with the layout.

On Friday, Jovi decided she could not hide at the orchard forever and went into town. After watching her pumpkin patch tenderly sprout, Jovi wanted to put a fence around the patch to keep the deer away. She hadn't noticed any prints yet, but Duchess had continued barking at night. Jovi wasn't sure it was deer Duchess was alarming to, but nonetheless, she didn't want anything getting into her pumpkins at such a vulnerable stage.

When she pulled up to the hardware store, she noticed a Lexus parked in the lot. It was not completely strange, although no one drove a vehicle like that locally, summer and tourist season was in full swing. Seeing vehicles that weren't a normal part of the landscape was par for the course in Woodsburrow during the summer. She got out and went inside. She grabbed her items and causally walked over to the office. She had only briefly talked to Steele since their farmers' market date. Jovi assumed he had been giving her some time to get the feeling of the Earth back under her after her incident with Nick. She had been really shaken up on Sunday. Jovi had shown her vulnerable side, which was not something she did with men, ever. Luke had called to let her know that her restraining order had been granted. It made her feel relieved, and she felt the shifting of power from Nick's court, back into her own. She wanted to let Steele know she was ok and invite him for a do over on their ice cream plans.

As she got to his office, however, she saw a woman talking to him. She brushed a hand to his arm and threw her head back in laughter. Jovi knocked on the door. "Hi Steele. I didn't know you would be busy today." Jovi said. Steele looked startled and stumbled back banging his knee on his desk while standing up from his chair. He rubbed at his knee and then ran a hand through his hair.

"Jovi, I hadn't heard anything back from my last message to you." He began.

The woman twirled around. "Hi there. I'm Stacey. How do you two know each other? I don't think I've seen you around before."

Stacey? What was she doing here, and why was she in Steele's office? "Steele and I are friends." Jovi stated as she took a step back retreating from this woman's overbearing spirit. "Steele has been helping me get acquainted to the town." Steele looked at her with a very confused look on his face. Stacey didn't seem to notice how uncomfortable they were and again laughed like she was being filmed by a camera crew.

"I call him the 'Unofficial Mayor.'" Steele had been right. This woman knew how to take up space. She didn't just take up space, she drowned everyone around her. Jovi wasn't about to stand here any longer.

"Just let me know when you aren't busy." Jovi said and headed for the door. If Steele wanted Stacey back, he could have her. She wasn't going to stand in his way. She would be no one's second choice.

"Jovi wait!" Steele called. But Jovi didn't turn around. She made her decision when she took a chance with Steele. It was time that he made his.

Jovi laid low that weekend. She had woken up to find a row of pumpkin plants destroyed. There were no deer tracks or any other tracks to be seen. *What had been messing with them?* Jovi couldn't afford to have her pumpkins destroyed. She got to work feverishly and spent the rest of the weekend installing her fence. It proved to be no easy task solo. Her arms and back ached, and her hands were full of blisters, but she was not going to chance this happening again. By the time the sun was setting on Sunday, she rushed to get her missing seedlings replanted. There would still be enough time for that row of pumpkins to catch up to the rest.

On Sunday night, Duchess and Jovi made a lasagna and played Michael Bublé. She hummed along while she sliced her tomatoes and swayed to the music. She drank a glass of her wine from another bottle she had picked up from the farmers' market. It was excellent. As she drank, she decided that she would make some hard cider with her heritage apples. She wouldn't be able to make it on time to sell it this year, but it would allow her some future growth options. It would be something new to add to Autumn Gold that might draw attention to a whole other set of customers.

Jovi loved how her daily life had changed since leaving her job in the city, and she was determined that she would be successful. She loved the orchard and the bond that she felt for the land, like it was a living breathing thing, and it grew stronger every day. Lynn had run the orchard until she had passed, and she had done a more than fine job up until then. If Lynn could succeed, Jovi would as well. Jovi was not going to sit around and pine for Steele. If he wanted to be with Stacey, then good for him. She had had her doubts that he was ready to move on to someone new.

***

She discovered that a volunteer group went around the downtown to paint, plant flowers, and just generally make it fresh before the influx of tourists and summer festivities were in full swing. She had been looking for ways to volunteer and connect to the community that she had planted herself in. So, Jovi met the group in front of the library at 8:00. She loved that her self-employed hours allowed her to participate in town activities on a Monday morning. Her work schedule in the city barely allowed her to attend doctor's appointments.

The group was made up of mostly retirees, none of whom she knew. That was pretty predictable for the timing of the event. Jovi picked up trash while the ladies, and a few men gossiped about the new babies that had been born, new marriages that were planned, and ones that were not predicted to last. *How did these people know what was happening behind these unfortunate souls' doors?* Apparently, Margret had been found in bed with the carpenter that was redoing her living room floor. Joe had been quick to kick her to the curb. Julie was pregnant with her sixth, and it was said that this one wasn't her husband's, but then again, neither was number four.

Jovi worked in silence. She drowned out their voices with her task at hand. Then, she heard Steele's name mentioned. "Did you hear Stacey was back in town?" "Oh Stacey, she was always such a nice girl." "I heard someone saw her talking with Steele." "Yes, Joanne was shopping and caught a glimpse of them." "Well, everyone knows those two are meant to be. They are cute as a button together. Steele with his dark handsome looks and Stacey with her blonde hair and light delicate features. They will make beautiful babies someday."

Jovi thought that she didn't care what Steele had decided, but the sound of his name made her stomach sour. A few of the men glanced up at her during the exchange as if to gauge her reaction to the news. Well, Jovi was not giving them that satisfaction. She wanted to volunteer and cleaning up the Main Street was something she was glad was being done, but she would need to find a less chatty group to volunteer with in the future.

Jovi drove home to find Hannah's Bug parked in her driveway. Hannah was nowhere to be seen, but Jovi knew she would find her inside with Duchess. She hadn't known she was coming, but she wasn't surprised she was here.

Hannah and Duchess were in the kitchen baking. *What was that divine smell?* Jovi took a giant inhale as she entered the front door. "Hannah?" She called. Hannah popped her head out of the kitchen.

"Ok listen," Hannah began. "I know that you aren't used to the best friend thing yet. But let me just clarify that when your boyfriend is seen by the town talking to his ex and you walk in and see? You then call me so I can give you some support."

"I don't want to wallow over Steele." Jovi said tossing her stuff down.

"Wallowing, trash talking, ignoring, I don't care how you want to deal, but you don't get to do it alone." Jovi smiled. Hannah just got her. She knew how to peel back her layers. "Now, I'm making a Dark Chocolate Fudge cake, and we are going to talk."

"I'll get the wine." Jovi replied.

As she gave Hannah the details about what had been happening, she started with her run in with Nick at the farmers' market. "You haven't seen him since, right?" Jovi shook her head no.

"I haven't. I'm hopeful that the restraining order is embarrassing enough to keep him away, plus Steele had threatened to kill him." Hannah's eyes got wide.

"I've never seen Steele mad like that. He is usually so levelheaded and in control."

"He was angry, and I was thankful. I've never had someone be so aggressive and physical with me. I was afraid for what Nick might do next." She shivered.

"This really doesn't sound like Steele has any intentions of being with Stacey. He fought a man off for you!" Hannah pointed out.

"And then I cried. I cried for an hour, huge sobs. My eyes were puffy for the next two days. He probably thinks I'm just some unstable emotional wreck."

Hannah shook her head. "I don't think so."

"Well, we hadn't talked much after. I stayed close to home until the restraining order was granted, and I didn't feel so shaky. When I went into town, there he was, in his office with Stacey all over him."

"But you don't know that he wanted her there."

"I don't want there to even be a hint of doubt in his head. I will not be a consolation prize. My mom created me with a man she thought loved her, but whatever it was wasn't enough to make him love me too. A love with conditions isn't love. I won't make that mistake with a man. I've dated to have some company and to fill in the lonely nights. Steele doesn't feel like just company, he feels like something more. If he wants to be with me, he has to have intentions that match mine. I have enough good company in my life now days."

Hannah looked at Jovi. "I completely agree that he needs to get his head in the direction he is going before he heads there. He must choose you or Stacy. I get why you feel that way. There are so many disappointing men in the world who don't put their head and their heart above the thing between their legs, but I don't think Steele is like that. I really don't think he wants to be with Stacey. Have you met her? She is very overwhelming just to listen to in a casual conversation. He also wouldn't move away from his family and the store. Stacey has made it clear to everyone she passes on the street that she doesn't want to stay here. I don't know why she was here, but I'm sure it was just temporary. I really think Steele is just worried about spooking you or messing things up." Jovi started to speak. Hannah interrupted. "Jovi just think about it. Ok? You don't have to forgive him and go begging him to come back, but you need to think about what you might say if you are the one he wants. You are already writing him off like the causal nobodies you dated in the city. You already said you know this is different. When we let ourselves really love someone and let them see our true selves, it's scary to have so much in another person's hands. Luke knows more about me than anyone on the planet. Arguments with him are the worst, not because he is mean and nasty, but because feeling rejected by that person feels like a rejection of who you are."

Hannah was right. She was making his decision for him and that wasn't fair. Jovi was becoming more than aware of the deep feelings she was developing for Steele. She was terrified she would be hurt. She was afraid of how his opinion might change of her as he got to know her better. She was full of fears.

Hannah and Jovi ate enough cake to make them sleepy, then, Hannah left. Jovi felt like she might explode if she didn't lie down and take a nap. She curled on the green couch, warm from the sun rays and Duchess, and she fell asleep.

Chapter 11

She woke to find herself still on the green couch. *What time was it?* Her precious clock told her that it was 6:30 AM. She needed to clear her head and took a walk outside to do so. She slipped on her boots, and Duchess followed Jovi out the door.

She walked outside and saw the most phenomenal sunrise. The red hues spread over the sky as daylight began to grow. It was chilly and damp, but the birds sang out with appreciation for another day. Being outside, quieted the restlessness in her soul. There was nothing like it in the world. Jovi and Duchess walked the path that she had mapped out and was starting to clear for the hayrides. They spooked some deer in the woods and saw some turkeys roosting in trees. She couldn't believe how large a wild turkey was! *How did something so large and noisy pass by humans daily without being spotted?* Duchess chases a few rabbits on the way back, and by the time she had returned, daylight had completely broke. Duchess was so happy they were starting out the day this way.

Jovi had to spend most of the morning weeding which was turning out to be her least favorite part of gardening. She had found old straw bales that she spread out in her pumpkin patch and vegetable garden. She hoped that would help with her weed problem. Then again, she knew she still had a lot to learn about how to garden efficiently and like a professional.

Her hands dirty and her cup filled, she went inside to make an omelet. She had cut fresh chives. She mixed the chives with the farm fresh brown eggs and topped it with artisan cheese. It was divine and went perfectly with her morning cup of coffee. All she was missing was some sourdough bread. She made a note to stop by Hannah's later in the week for some.

Jovi called her mother and invited her up for a visit. She was thrilled that Jovi was calling and couldn't wait to see the property. They decided that she would visit the weekend after the Fourth of July. Her mother wanted to spend some solo time with Jovi, and Jovi was excited to share all the things she had been building and discovering about herself, with her mom. She knew she would love it.

Since she was making phone calls, which was absolutely not her favorite thing to do, she decided to call the folk band, The River Runners, from the market and book them to play for September 1st. They were a reasonable price, and she was thrilled to have them set the mood. Jovi called the Fat Hippo food truck and asked them to come as well. That pulled pork sandwich she had gotten had been divine, not to mention the smells that wafted from the BBQ sauce and smoked meats were heavenly. She was quite sure she had fallen in love with that sandwich. Satisfied that she had done enough planning for the day, she grabbed Duchess and loaded her up in the car.

They drove around for a while, just enjoying the day and seeing new areas she hadn't before. Since leaving the city and that job, she had spent more time awakened and immersed in life around her. She watched sunrises and sunsets, and not just glanced at them. She smiled at her neighbors on the street and knew them by name. She watched and listened to patterns of the birds near her home. She observed clouds and the changes in the plant life around her as the seasons gradually changed. It made her feel like more than just a robot completing tasks. It made her feel alive. She had been watching the same things happening within herself. She was learning about the things she disliked, like cold coffee and wet feet. She was understanding more of the things that she liked. She loved old books and old movies. She loved gardening and a glass of wine in the evening. She loved the color green and being in the kitchen. She noticed her high energy in the morning and slump after lunch. She noticed how Hannah made her feel freer. Her energy was infectious. And she certainly hadn't missed the absolute rush and weightlessness that Steele gave her. She didn't want to lose that feeling, and she didn't want to stop getting to know herself here.

After driving for a while, they ended up at Lost Lake just a few miles from her own house. Duchess bounded out of the car into the water and Jovi sat down on the beach. Today was the first truly uncomfortable warm day of the year, and she was thankful they had finished the outside work early when the morning was crisp. The beach and its natural coolness were a perfect way to spend the afternoon. Duchess was happily splashing in the water, but she knew to stay close by. She was such an intelligent dog. Jovi was grateful. There were a few other families with little kids down on the other side of the beach laughing and running around. She smiled. Despite the chatty old people and the creep, this town was a great town to grow up in.

The community was tight knit. The people were mostly kind and good. There were always fun events and support. Jovi thought it was the perfect place to raise children. Her thoughts were interrupt by someone calling her name.

"Jovi? Jovi!" She turned her head around to see Steele with a fishing pole in his hand and a bucket hat on his head. Despite being angry with him, the sight made her giggle uncontrollably. He looked up and down at himself and smiled back. "I know, I'm a dork. I told you I like fishing."

"It's cute." She grinned. "I'm glad you are spending some time fishing."

"We need to talk," he said. She nodded at him and patted the sand next to her. Duchess made her way over. She was super wet and as her tail wagged it spread small droplets of water everywhere. Steele somehow ignored the tsunami being caused by the small furry creature and gave her the most enthusiastic greeting. Jovi's heart swelled and felt broken all at once. She wanted him to be hers, only. Just because she wanted it, however, didn't make it true.

"Where have you been Jovi? I told you I was all in. I sat by your side on the floor with you while you cried. Why did you disappear? What did I do wrong?" Jovi looked at him.

"Stacey was back and in your office. You two looked awful cozy." She said.

"Stacey was back, yes, and taking up space like a rhinoceros as usual. I told her I have no interest in being with her ever again. I told you that I didn't want her back. Why didn't you believe me?"

"I don't want to be a runner up." She replied. "I don't want you to be with me and compare me to someone else or wish I was someone else. I've never been so candid about myself or my feelings before, ever. I don't need who I am to not be enough for you."

"Runner up?" Steele held his hand to his head. "Runner up?" He repeated. "You are the first-place prize and the whole celebration cake too. Jovi, I've never met a woman as determined and as true to themselves as you are. You are independent and selfless, intuitive and the most gorgeous woman I've ever laid eyes on. I want you, only you." She took a deep breath and decided to try bluntness, since whatever approach she had been attempting so far wasn't working.

"Steele, I'm scared. I've never been with anyone that I actually gave a crap either way if it works out or not. I've never been around a couple long enough to see what a serious relationship looks like and how it functions. My mom raised me alone. I didn't have men in and out of my life, there just wasn't one. I care about what happens between us. Every time you are near me, I feel like a missing piece of myself has arrived, and I don't want it to leave. It's scary to have that piece not connected to my own body. You make me feel like I need something that I can't give to myself or create by myself. I'm scared to need someone like that, Steele."

Steele moved closer to her. "You don't need to be afraid of being with me, Jovi. I've been alone long enough to know myself and exactly what I want. I'm certain that's you. I've watched my parents love each other my whole life. They stayed together through rough times at the store, Dad's stroke, the death of their parents, fights, you name it. They are still in love after all these years. I want that. I want to look at my partner in 30 years and say you are my best friend and favorite person on the planet. You are an extension of myself that makes me the best version. I can lead us there. You don't have to have it all figured out." He reached for Jovi's hand, and she took it. The worn leather feeling that had begun to feel familiar and comforting. "Please let me back in. Trust me." Jovi leaned in and kissed him with all the passion she was feeling in her chest. He grabbed her face and pulled her close.

"I don't know what is happening here, but I don't think I can stop it even if I try." She whispered.

***

Jovi woke the next morning with a huge grin on her face. She had never been kissed as well as Steele kissed her, and her entire night had been filled with dreams beneath the sheets with Steele. A stark difference from the restless nights she had been having. Steele was coming over this morning in his truck so they could stop by a few artisans who already had items for her fall opening. They were going to stop by the Grant's as well. Caroline had called to invite her over to check in, and she wanted to talk to Charlie about the tractor tires.

She took Duchess out for their run and jumped in the shower. She was running behind and was giddy to have Steele in her house again. When he arrived at 9:00 sharp, *(Was this man ever late?)* she was just pulling on her jeans and hurried down the stairs to get the door. Duchess was barking wildly. "Sorry." She said as she answered the door haphazardly. "I'm not quite ready."

"That's ok." Steele said as he entered. "I'll wait." He sat on the couch with Duchess and stroked her back as she drifted deep into sleep. He waited patiently as she finished dressing and put on her make up. She loved that he wasn't restless and could just be still without her feeling like she needed to rush.

The men she had dated in the city were high strung all the time. No room for rest. No room for waiting. His calming personality was exactly what she needed. She re-entered the living room, no longer frazzled, but her heart still pounded from the memory of her dream last night. It was going to be a distracting day. She could remember in great detail what those lips felt like against hers and craved them once again.

When they got into Steele's truck, Steele had two cups of hot coffee waiting for them, cream and sugar in both. Jovi smiled and grabbed her cup. His love language at its finest. "Can we head to the Grant's first?" She asked. Steele nodded.

"Absolutely. That's a great friendship that you have made. I grew up with their sons in school. They were quite a bit older but some of the nicest guys. The Grants are one of the best families in town."

"Caroline reminds me of my grandmother, full of more spark though. I just adore them."

As they rode, Jovi told him about her volunteering experience. Steele nodded. "That group can be a little overwhelming. They love to gossip. It's probably fair to say they start most of it in this town. You should help set up for the Fourth of July and with running the concession stand. They always need people for that. The families from the farmers' market are the majority of the people that help there. They are a much friendlier bunch."

"I'll do that." She responded. She was glad there was volunteering she could do in town that didn't require her to put her opinion in on Katie and John's new marriage, and if she thought it would last.

The Grant farm was a flurry of activity. It reminded her of a hive of bees. Everyone buzzed around working toward the same goal. They had multiple employees who were in the fields picking both weeds and early strawberries. Others were milking in the barn. Charlie was in his element driving the tractor and mulching various plants. Caroline was in the front of the house. Jovi couldn't see what she was doing from the road. Duchess was in the backseat with her head out the window engrossed in the smells that were permeating her nose.

"Hello Jovi. Hi Steele. Is Duchess with you? Let that poor baby out." Jovi barely got the door opened while Duchess bounded out. She was in every puddle and dirt pile she could find. She would need a bath later, but for now, Duchess was living her best life. Duchess greeted Caroline like a best friend much like she had Hannah, before Steele and Jovi even stepped away from the truck. "You are a beautiful girl."

"She is the best dog. I've never had one before, but I'm certain she is the best. I tried to sneak a stray in one time, a grey mixed breed. My mom found out pretty quickly. I wasn't that good at lying. I cried buckets when she said we couldn't keep it and would have to give it to a shelter. We ended up taking the dog to my grandparent's place, and he lived out his days as my grandpa's best boy." Jovi smiled and rubbed Duchess between the ears.

"There is nothing like a good dog in your life." Caroline replied. "It's good for your soul. They are loyal to their owners always and are excellent judges of character. They know how to trust their instincts even when we don't." She smiled and they looked over at Duchess who was trying to wrangle Steele into fetch with a stick.

The Grant farm was a family operation, it functioned with the help of everyone. Steele saw two of Caroline's son's vehicles parked outside the barn. He went in to say hello and help them with chores. He was going to let Charlie know Jovi wanted to talk to him as well, so Jovi didn't have to chase him on the tractor. Jovi loved his willingness to help anyone and saw him roll up his sleeves and take off his coat before entering the barn. "A good man shows his affection through his actions." Caroline said watching her as Steele walk away. "You learn more about a person from how they treat others than you can from just the words they say." Jovi nodded.

"I've dated some men that were inappropriately rude to the wait staff at restaurants we attended together. I have no tolerance for that and was mortified by that behavior. Needless to say, there never was another date after that."

Caroline ushered Jovi to sit in the chairs she had set up outside. Jovi looked at what Caroline was up to. "Are you canning?" She asked. Caroline nodded.

"Strawberry jam. It gets too warm inside during the summer to run the stove all day, so I use my outdoor kitchen. The boys made it for me one year, and it's my favorite. I miss it during the winter. It's less mess to clean up, and I can keep tabs on the farm better." She winked. Caroline was very much the boss if one had to be crowned as such.

"You will have to teach me how. I would love to can some apple pie filling to sell this fall."

"I'd love to." Caroline said. "I'm blessed with two fine daughters-in-law, but I never had a daughter of my own."

She smiled. "Whatever I can do to help you Jovi, I always will." Caroline squeezed Jovi.

Jovi loved these people and this town. Despite her starting out as a tourist, she had been embraced by the community and claimed as one of their own. They chatted about the farm and how the growing season was going. Jovi asked some questions about watering and mulch. She made sure she gave Caroline a personal invitation to opening day. Having the Grants there would be important for her. "We wouldn't miss it. Charlie and I will be there. Charlie will want to give the hayrides you know."

"He is the only man I would want for the job."

"I see you and Steele are getting along quite well. How is that going?"

Jovi blushed. "Actually, it scares me how natural it is."

Caroline smiled. "You can still be an independent woman and love a man."

"That's a completely new concept to me." Jovi replied.

"Even the strongest of women, fall in love."

"Lynn never did." Jovi said. "She seemed to have a very full life."

Caroline's smile turned sad. "Lynn filled portions of her life very full because of a heart that never mended."

"What do you mean?"

"Lynn never had any children or married. That orchard was like her family. It was a shame though because every year when the school field trips visited her orchard, was when she lit up the most. Lynn was in love as a young woman. She was so smitten with the man. When we would spend our girl days together, she would gush about how perfect they were together. He cared about her building her orchard. He listened to her, and she thought they were in love. I thought it was odd that I never met him or ever saw them in public together. She was absolutely crushed when he proposed to someone else."

"What? That's horrible. Why?" Jovi asked.

"His family pushed him to be with someone who's family had money. That was what was most important to them, that he would be taken care of his whole life. The most important thing to the man was not letting his family down. Lynn had worked extremely hard to have what she built. Her father died when she and her siblings were small. Her mother supported them, but they were poor. She was a natural beauty though. She was well liked in school. No one teased her for being trash or anything like that. In fact, she was the prom queen. It was no surprise to me that a man with a bright future would have fallen for her. It broke my heart that he was too embarrassed by his affection to tell his parents or anyone else. Lynn never got over that. That same summer she planted her trees, she told me she was pregnant. He was supposed to tell his parents that he couldn't be with anyone but Lynn. She was thrilled both about the pregnancy and that he was finally standing up to his parents. She told me she would tell me his name after he told them. Not long after however, she lost the baby, and he was too much of a coward to tell anyone about them. He ended up getting married not long after, and not to Lynn. She grieved the loss of him and the baby for so long, I think she gave up on loving another human in that way. She poured all of that into the property. She was constantly developing recipes and planting her next generation of trees. She lived her life as happy as she believed she deserved. I always felt guilty having the boys and Charlie, while she was all alone." Caroline's eyes clearly showed the grief she held onto for the loss of her friend and the life of emptiness she had lived.

"Don't ever limit your own happiness Jovi. Don't be afraid of love and heartbreak like Lynn was. We all make mistakes. She was a wonderful woman who deserved everything she wanted." Jovi nodded. She understood what it was like to live in a subdued form of happiness. She had told herself what she should want or what she should do for years. She was glad to be breaking that pattern and excited for what was ahead.

Charlie ambled over, having talked to Steele, and parked his tractor to talk with Jovi. "Hey kid!" He called. "It's great to see you." He hugged her in greeting. "You need my help with something?"

"Well, I noticed a few weeks ago, that all four of my tractor tires are completely flat. I tried inflating them, but none of them would take air. I'm sure I just don't know exactly what I'm doing. I'm hoping you can come take a look and get them fixed up before hayrides and harvest this fall."

Charlie frowned. "All four are flat?" Jovi nodded. "That's odd. Did you drive it after we were there last?" Jovi shook her head no. "They shouldn't be flat then. They all looked in great condition when I was there. In fact, I made sure they were inflated and ready to go after I ran the tractor. I'll come take a look this week."

"I also wanted to ask if you want to do the hayrides on opening day?"

"I would love to." He responded with a giant smile.

Steele came over with Duchess who had managed to get herself dirtier than Jovi could have imagined. Caroline brought Jovi the hose and some soap, and she hosed her down. There was no way she could get into the truck as dirty as she was. After Duchess got her royal treatment, they got into the truck and drove away with Duchess snoozing in the backseat.

Chapter 12

Jovi and Steele spent the rest of the day picking up candles, coffee cups, rugs, and paintings. Jovi enjoyed every visit they made. Each artisan wanted to show her what they were working on now and what they had made for her in great detail. She loved listening to them speak about why they had used certain techniques or colors. Some of the pieces had stories about places they had been, people they loved, or something inspirational they had heard. Jovi loved how artists saw the world, and each item she picked up to place in the back of Steele's truck was truly something special. She had only gotten through a quarter of the visits she would need to make, but she was already blown away. Steele made sure all the items were nestled snug into the back, and they headed for ice cream.

"Isn't it so amazing how they can see things people walk by every day and turn them into a work of art?"

Steele nodded. "I've always admired artists with craft skills. I can draw, and I taught myself to do steelwork, but it's amazing to watch them make pottery and leatherworks and rag rugs."

"It really is. I have limited artistic skills, but my mother is a remarkable artist. I had always been transfixed watching her take a blank piece of canvas and turning it into a place that had so much detail I could picture myself there. It was just like magic. She goes into such a trance when she paints." Jovi smiled. Her mom was an extremely influential person in her life. She had always wanted to be just like her.

"Your mom sounds like an incredible human being. I know she must be to have created a woman like you."

"She's actually coming up the weekend after the big Fourth of July bash. We are going to get some alone time together. We haven't gotten that in years. You could stop in for dinner a night and meet her if you wanted."

He looked at her. "Yeah?"

"I mean if that isn't weird for you." Jovi said looking down.

"No, not at all. Jovi, don't do that." He said grabbing her hand. "Don't take a chance and then reel it back. I want to meet her. Okay?"

She nodded and smiled. "Okay."

They had finished their ice creams by the time they got to the orchard. Duchess jumped out of the car rejuvenated from her nap. Jovi grabbed one of the boxes of candles and carried it towards the barn. She almost dropped them when she saw it. Steele was right behind her with another box. The words "Go home whore" were spray painted in bright red on the aged wood. She looked around and saw that her fence she had spent an entire weekend on, was destroyed. The scene in front of her made her sick. *Who had done this?*

"We need to call Luke." Steele said. He pulled Jovi close, whistled for Duchess, and whipped out his phone remaining forcibly calm. "He is on duty today."

Luke arrived in less than 10 minutes. Jovi knew he had come quicker than the typical response time. He was worried. "Jovi are you ok?" He asked as he power walked towards them.

"I'm fine." She said. "Steele and I just got home." Steele and Luke did one of those bro hugs complete with patting.

"Let's go and get you inside with Duchess. I'll clear the house first. Then Steele and I will walk around to make sure there isn't any other damage. I don't want you putting yourself through unnecessary risk. Whoever did this has zeroed in on you as a target. They are obviously incredibly angry." Jovi nodded. Her hands were shaking. She felt violated yes, but also furious. She had worked hours and hours and poured out her own blood, sweat, and tears to have gotten where she was. *What did she do that upset this person so much?*

Jovi paced around the house with Duchess while the boys checked the property. She had calmed to a reasonable level of anger when they came back. "No other damage was done." Luke reported. "Is there anyone you think might be responsible?" Steele and Luke settled into the sitting room. Luke sat in a chair across from Jovi and Steele sat on the green couch with Jovi and Duchess.

"Well," Jovi began, "there is Nick. You know about the run ins I've had with him. I know Hannah had said he is unlikely to take no well, but I haven't seen him since the restraining order, and he has never bothered me at home before." Jovi said.

Luke nodded. "He isn't a character who is apt to change. I've had complaints of sexual advances from him before, but never vandalism. It's not impossible though. Is there anyone else?"

"There was a woman." Jovi stated.

Steele looked at her puzzled. "What woman?" He asked.

"I don't know. She was older maybe in her 50s? She cornered me at the farmers' market and told me I should think again about my choices and that I have no business digging up old graves."

"Steele did you see who it was?" Luke asked him.

Steele shook his head. "I don't remember this happening at all. Jovi, why didn't you say anything?" Steele asked.

Jovi shrugged. "She disappeared so fast after she threatened me. I couldn't find her in a crowd to have you tell me who she was. You were talking to a customer of yours, and I didn't want to interrupt. I felt like the whole town was judging me for being out with you that day, and I didn't want to look unhinged or who knows what all the gossipers would say. Then Nick attacked me and that seemed a lot more pressing than some random lady."

"Have you seen her anywhere since?" Luke asked Jovi.

She shook her head. "I haven't, and I've been keeping an eye out."

"Have you noticed anything else strange?" He asked.

Jovi paused to think. "Well," she began, "there had been some odd things happening, but at the time they didn't seem like red flags for anything." She saw Steele run his hand through his hair out of her peripheral vision. "For starters, I asked Charlie today about my tractor tires. All four were flat one morning, and I can't get them to inflate. He still needs to check them over, but he was concerned. He said they had been in good condition when he left. He was the last to drive it. He seems pretty meticulous, especially when it comes to machinery."

Luke nodded. "He is definitely known for his machinery skills around here."

"I also had an entire row of pumpkin plants destroyed. I looked for prints. I had been worried about deer, but there weren't any anywhere. That's when I installed the fence. I had a delivery go missing a few weeks back. The post office was insistent it had been delivered here, but the box was nowhere to be found. It was a large box, so it was not something that could have been just misplaced. I've noticed Duchess has been barking at night. It's not every night, but a few times a week it happens. Again, another reason why I was worried it might be deer. I usually flip on the lights and take her outside though, and we've never seen any animals out there when we do. We live in the country, so animals aren't uncommon to her. She is more apt to bark at humans."

"Anything else?" He asked.

"Not that I can think of." Jovi replied.

"I agree, any one of those things individually could easily be overlooked, but that's a lot of poor luck for someone who has only lived here a month. I think you should consider security cameras if you can."

Jovi nodded. "I think that's a good suggestion."

"I wouldn't stay here alone tonight if you can help it. It's unlikely the culprit would come back twice in the same night, but with how fixated this person is on you, it wouldn't be a good idea to chance that either. We will start doing some patrolling out here on the night shift. That seems to be when most of the trouble is occurring. The night shift guys are always looking for something exciting on slow nights. If any other damage pops up or we notice the violence escalating, we will need to re-evaluate how to keep you the safest."

Jovi put her head in her hands. "I don't have time for this." She groaned.

"I'll help you get caught up." Steele said.

"We will make sure you are safe and ready for opening day."

She needed to get some rest and figure out how much damage was done and deal with the clean up quickly. She had an orchard to open.

After Luke left, Jovi got up to make some tea. Steele followed her into the kitchen. She turned around abruptly and blurted out, "Will you stay tonight? I could go to Hannah's if you don't want to, but I'm so tired and so shook up. I would rather you stay here with me."

"I'll stay. Someone needs to watch over you and Duchess." He pulled her into a tight, long embrace and kissed the top of her head. "Tomorrow, we will fix the fence. I'll come up with something for the barn. I think we should ask Charlie to come look at the tires too. It would be good to know if that is part of the damage that has been caused." Jovi nodded. It was so good to have someone else make decisions and have a plan. Her brain was too rattled to think.

Jovi and Steele sat at the kitchen and drank the piping hot tea. Even though Jovi knew that the temperature of the air was not exactly "cold" she felt frozen to her core. The heat from the tea permeated her hands and seeped into her bones. She shivered.

Steele had noticed and looked at her. "Everything ok?"

"I'm just ready for bed." She replied.

They headed upstairs and Jovi could feel the tension between though like an electrical current. She changed in the bathroom, anxious about what Steele was thinking on the other side of the door. She came out and saw him with his shirt off and thinking came to a halt. All the words drifted right out of her brain into the air. She stood staring at Steele. "I'm sorry." He ran his hand through his hair. *That must be a nervous tick.* Jovi thought. "I usually sleep-in boxers at home. I'd wear whatever you want me to make you more comfortable, but I spent time in the Grant's barn today. I don't want to lay down on your yellow sheets like this. Do you mind if I shower quick?" She was about to remind him that she worked outside in the dirt all day and of the dog she owned that constantly rolled in everything, but she could smell the scent of cows on his clothing. She wrinkled her nose and nodded. "My grandma would roll over in her grave if she thought I was acting like a slob to the woman I was dating."

Jovi giggled and kissed him on the cheek. "Help yourself." She gestured to the master bath.

Jovi grabbed the clothes Steele had left on the floor while he jumped in the shower. She figured their best option was to throw them in the wash. If he planned on staying in the morning, he would want clean clothes. Jovi started the washing machine and considered if she had anything for him to wear that evening. She rummaged through her drawers to find the boxers that said "Working hard? Or Hardly working?" that she got as a gag gift during a Christmas gift exchange when she first started her job in the city. She wasn't sure why she had kept it after moving, especially with all the donations she had made prior to packing. Whatever the reason, she was grateful to have something covering the beautiful body that was going to be beside her all night. Anything to help temper the temptation. She slipped into the bathroom one more time to place the boxers on the sink and slipped out.

Jovi and Duchess settled into bed in their usual positions while Steele finished his shower. The rush she felt in her chest from knowing that man was completely naked on the other side of the door, made her crazy. She tried to think of something else and thoughts about the words on her barn, and the way Nick had treated her floated into her head. *Another person's opinion of myself does not make it true*, she reminded herself, but it did make her want to be meticulous with her relationship with Steele. Everyone gossiped with too much vigor. She was a small business owner and so was Luke in the very same community. She knew if they were to break up, it would be discussed at length all over town. It was probably being discussed this very minute. She heard the shower handle turning the water off, and she inhaled again. *Pull it together, Jovi.* She thought loudly to herself.

Steele emerged from the bathroom with the office boxers on. "Where did you get these things?" He asked.

"A Christmas party gag gift. I have no idea why I kept them, but they turned out to be more useful than I thought." Jovi laughed. He smiled and then stared at Jovi intensely for only a second before he turned out the lights. He grabbed the quilt that was on the plush Victorian chair in the corner of the room and crawled into bed at her side. Despite all the feelings his half naked presence in her bed stirred up, she felt safe with him there. They laid there for a while, extra space between them to cool their imaginations. Both of them laid very still and breathed slowly, but clearly still awake. It wasn't long before his calming presence and the even sound of his breath took over and lulled Jovi to sleep.

Even though they had fallen asleep on separate side of the bed, and Steele had wrapped himself in that quilt like it was a shield, they woke up completely intertwined with each other. The quilt lay somewhere on the floor. Jovi had never slept with another man all night. Being with Steele this morning made her never want to leave the bed. "Good morning, beautiful." Steele mumbled into her hair. "Coffee?"

Jovi giggled. "Yes, coffee definitely is my love language."

"Where are my clothes?" He asked.

"In the washing machine." She replied "I'll run them in the dryer. It shouldn't take long."

He headed downstairs wearing just the boxers to ramble through her kitchen. By the time Jovi got dressed, the coffee was ready, and Duchess was outside exploring. Steele grabbed his clothes from the dryer, and they went to have coffee on the porch. Jovi loved that they could sit in comfortable silence. They were both people who liked to observe the world around them and effortlessly gave each other space for their thoughts.

They finished their cups and immediately got to work on the fence. Jovi had left a message with Caroline who said that Charlie would be over today between chores to check on the tires. She was genuinely concerned about the problems that had been occurring and offered anything they could give. Jovi had declined but thanked her and said she wouldn't hesitate to call if she did need more.

With more than one person, fixing the fence only took a few hours. Jovi was amazed at how much lighter the workload was. They moved over to the barn and stared at the letters. After a long pause, Steele finally spoke. "Well, I think it's obvious what the solution is." Jovi looked over at him bewildered.

"It is?" She asked. He nodded.

"I need to paint your logo and company name over the spot."

"Can you do that?"

He nodded. "I told you I can draw, but I can paint as well. We will have to run into town to grab some paint though."

After a quick run to town where Jovi had chosen a mustard yellow background with black drawing and lettering, they were back at it. Jovi watched as Steele created magic on the horrible words, just like her mother would. He cautiously drew out his word and slowly started to paint. Her mighty trees and giant apple came alive with the words Autumn Gold Orchard overlapping it. People would see it as they entered the orchard barn and would think she had good attention to detail. To Jovi, it felt like she was saying to the vandal, I'm not going anywhere. And she felt pride. They would figure out who was causing all this damage. Whoever it was intended on scaring her out of town, and she had no intentions of leaving.

Charlie arrived later that afternoon. Steele had already left for the day; he had some work to do at the store. Jovi was happy to have Charlie there. Although she didn't feel as frazzled as she had felt last night, she was still spooked. "Let's take a look, kid." Charlie said. He grabbed his bag and they headed over to the tractor. He carefully inspected the tires. "Hmm." He said. "Just like I had thought. The tires are in good condition. The material is not in a poor enough state to be spontaneously ripping." He grabbed the air compressor and tried to inflate them. After carefully watching how each one reacted, he spoke. "Jovi, someone poked a hole in every one of these. This was intentional. I can patch them, but make sure you let Luke know that this is part of your vandalism problem." He looked at her. "It makes me angry that someone is doing this to you. I know Luke will do his job, but you are always welcome in our spare bedroom. Duchess as well." He patted Duchess' head.

Jovi nodded. "Thank you, Charlie. I don't want them to think I'll be scared off of my property though."

"I understand, but don't try to be a hero either." Jovi smiled and left him to fix the tires.

Chapter 13

Weeks had passed without any more damage occurring to Jovi's property. The police officers drove by most nights, and Duchess had been barking less often. She had ordered security cameras, but they hadn't arrived yet. She would need some help installing them when they did. She couldn't believe the Fourth of July was already this weekend. *How did summers always go by so fast?* Jovi was helping set up for the festival today. She hoped for a better experience than her last time volunteering and was bringing some deviled eggs and chips for people to snack on while they worked. When she arrived, she knew some of the people as vendors from the market. Hannah was there too. She was not about to let Jovi be thrown to the gossip wolves, just in case it wasn't as great as Steele had thought it would be. Hannah set out her cookies and Jovi set down her chips and eggs.

The day was amazing. Families with children were there, farmers and some grandparents who had been helping with set up for years. They played music and the kids ran and danced. People laughed. The atmosphere was friendly and inviting. People came and went throughout the day, but help was plentiful. At the end of the day everything looked perfect for the event. Jovi had found her group of people. She had already exchanged numbers with a few of the ladies. One of them worked for the food pantry, and Jovi offered to run a food drive at Autumn

Gold that fall. She wanted to show this community the same kindness it had showed her.

Jovi and Hannah had signed up to run the concession stand in the morning on Saturday. They were going to spend the rest of the day enjoying the festival together before the guys showed up. Jovi enjoyed meeting more of the town and everyone she talked to seemed genuinely happy she was opening Autumn Gold back up. They handed out French fries and fresh doughnuts. Hannah had brought twenty Kringles and sold out of them in the first hour. They were on their third giant pot of coffee by the time their shift was over.

Hannah and Jovi spent the day playing all the silly carnival games and eating every carnival food known to man. They laughed and chatted. "So, have you guys slept together yet?" Hannah had been asking regularly for the last week now.

"No." Jovi replied. "Steele wants to take it slow. I think we are spending more energy trying not to sleep with each other than anything else."

"I think you two are overthinking this. Sexual compatibility is just as important as good communication."

Jovi nodded. "I agree. I invited him to meet my mom. I'd like to know that we don't have a doomed relationship because we aren't good together in bed."

"Maybe he is waiting for you to be ready after the advances you had from Nick. Why can't you make the first move?"

They decided to ride the Ferris wheel at the end of the day. They could see over the entire town. It looked like a real-life painting with the sun beginning to set beyond it. Its colors were on vibrant display as they spread across the sky. The guys would be meeting them here soon. "I'm so stuffed I don't think I'll need to eat for weeks." Hannah said letting her head fall back. Jovi peered down at the crowd.

"Hannah?" She asked. "Who is that?"

"Who are you talking about?" Hannah said as she leaned forward and scanned the crowd below them.

"The woman with the long sundress that looks like the American flag and giant floppy white hat." Hannah found her almost immediately. The outfit the woman was wearing made her stick out like a sore thumb.

"That's Nancy Webster, the richest woman in town. Her husband Richard owns a chain of hotels including the Aspen Inn and Suites in town. Her daughter is…" But Hannah didn't get to finish her sentence. Stacey strode up to her mother's side with a large lemonade in hand.

"Stacey." Jovi finished. "Why do you ask? It's definitely typical for her to be strolling around town dressed like she wants the world staring at her. I can see her cleavage from up here."

"That's the woman that threatened me at the farmers' market." Jovi replied.

Hannah turned to look at her. "Are you sure?" Jovi nodded. "Maybe she was just upset about hearing you were with Steele. I'm sure she is over it now." As she spoke, Jovi and Hannah could see the men approaching the Ferris wheel deep in conversation with each other. Their path directly crossed Nancy and Stacey. Both women went up to them and spoke with what Jovi was sure they thought was charm. Both women touched the men as they spoke and stood squarely in their path. Steele and Luke's body language made it clear they were uncomfortable and wanting to leave. They finally had side stepped around them when the girls got off the ride.

"What did Nancy have to say?" Hannah asked Luke.

He shrugged. "They flittered with Steele and told me how handsome I looked in my uniform. They seemed pretty delirious about the fact that Steele is no longer with Stacey. Nancy invited Steele over for dinner, and Stacey said she would see him later."

Jovi locked eyes with Steele. "I told them no thank you and wished them a good evening." He shrugged. "I think Stacey was a little shocked. She isn't used to hearing the word no."

"Nancy is the woman I saw at the farmers' market." Both men turned and looked at Jovi.

"Are you certain?"

Jovi nodded. "She is pretty hard to miss now that I've seen her a second time."

Luke agreed. "That she is. She makes it clear she likes it that way too."

The four walked away, Jovi and Steele holding hands and Luke with his arm around Hannah's shoulders, to find a place where they would watch the fireworks. Jovi glanced backwards to see Nancy glaring at her.

As they sat on the blankets waiting for the fireworks to begin, Jovi thought about how much she loved this group of humans. They had spent the last hour handing out fliers for her opening day. Each one genuinely cared about the other and gave of themselves generously. Although Jovi had never had best friends before, she never wanted to be without them again. They made life so much brighter, and lighter. Even with the vandalism and rumors, Jovi felt like she was where she belonged. In the end, everything would be alright, and she wouldn't have to face any of it alone. She looked at Hannah. She had the sunniest personality. It reminded her of her mom's which was probably what had drawn Jovi to her in the first place. Hannah's personality shone twice as bright with Luke around her. Jovi hoped someone would see her shining with Steele as well. She certainly felt light warming her from the inside out when he was around. He had shown her consistency, big-heartedness, dedication, and patience. Those were all qualities she wanted in a true partner. The safety she felt when he sat beside her and the faith in her dreams that she pursued were things that she never imagined another human might do for her.

They watched the display over Lost Lake. It was the best one Jovi had seen in years. Red fireworks would shatter across the sky and then float down as if they were in slow motion. The blue would explode loudly. The night sky was clear and full of stars. It couldn't have been a more perfect night, and Jovi started to yawn. The warmth she felt from Steele and the fullness of the last two days made her feel exhausted. There was still a parade to attend in the morning. After the third yawn, Steele offered to bring her home and she agreed. Jovi hugged Hannah tight. "Thank you for being the best, best friend."

"Always." Hannah answered back. "I'll meet you at the bakery in the morning. You bring the coffee, and I'll have the doughnuts." She winked. Jovi knew she would want all the details from how her night had gone with Steele.

On the ride back to her house, Jovi decided that Hannah was right. Steele and Jovi had built a relationship on friendship and kindness, but they needed to be lovers as well. *Otherwise, what made that different than her friendship with Hannah and Luke?* If there wasn't enough spark in the bedroom, they shouldn't continue dating. But at the same time, she couldn't stop picturing him naked, and it was clouding her judgement on just about everything else. She couldn't imagine how someone who made her feel like she had been hit with a bolt of electricity every time he touched her would not do the same in the bedroom, but she wanted to find out just the same.

When Steele parked the car, Jovi leaned in to kiss him. It was the most passion fueled kissed she had ever had in her life. He grabbed her and pulled her closer to him. His touch was gentle, but she could also feel the insistence in his strength. It was as if he was claiming her as his. He kissed her again. It left her immediately wanting more. She moved her hands into that long dark hair he was always pushing back. Then she ran her hands down into his shirt and over his strong and wide shoulders. He guided her on top of him and traced his fingertips along her stomach. When his fingertips had reached her side, he slid his hands down into the pocket of her jeans and grasped her. They couldn't keep their hands off each other as their breathing quickened. "Jovi." Steele whispered. "I know you've never been with a good man before. Let me warn you that the differences are not limited to outside of the bedroom."

"Is that a promise?" Jovi teased back her face pressed up against his. "Will you come in?" She asked.

He looked at her. "Do you want me to? I thought you were tired."

She shook her head. "Not anymore." Jovi grinned.

They climbed the stairs in silence and entered her bedroom. Steele had not been up to her room since the vandalism but having him in there tonight felt just as natural as it had when she had needed him for protection and support. Today she needed something else entirely. They stood with an extra wide gap between them. The only hint that Steele was nervous was the hand that went through his dark brown hair.

He looked her up and down. "Are you sure you are ready for this Jovi?" He asked.

"Are you?" She asked back with a twinkle in her eye. With those words spoken, the dam that had been barely holding back the flood broke wide open. Steele careful grabbed the hem of Jovi's shirt and moving extra slowly with his hands brushing against her skin, guided the shirt off over Jovi's head. He traced her shoulder with his hands so gently her body lit up with goosebumps, and she shivered. She yanked at his shirt until it slid over his head and traced his muscles in his chest down to his stomach. She replaced her hands with her mouth and followed the path she had just created. He was such a handsome naked man. His body was strong and felt good to be lying against a man who used his body more primitively than the men in the city. The only physical activity they ever did was lifting weights at the local gym. Their hands were always soft, like they had applied lotion that morning. Their bodies were always unnaturally sun kissed from a tanning booth. Steele's body conveyed so much more. His strong shoulders and tight abs were built by moving things at the store, by lifting heavy metal that he manipulated into works of art, by the help that he constantly showed his neighbors, that he had shown her. This strong body was used to build up this community he loved so much. His hands were worn like a nice leather, and the phantom texture it left behind on her skin drove her wild.

He pulled her close and traced a line of kisses behind her ear down to her chest and repeated on the other side. Despite their urgent need, Steele was going to take his time. His hands followed the edge of her bra, and slowly, he reached behind her to remove it. Jovi shimmied it to the floor. Jovi fumbled with the belt holding his pants up. When she finally released it, they dropped loudly on the ground. Steele unbuttoned her pants and peeled them from her body. He paused and grabbed her hand and led her to the bed. He wasn't kidding that good men were better in the bedroom. She had never been loved so tenderly and thoroughly. It was as if he was memorizing every inch of her body and how every touch made her respond. His only goal was her pleasure. It wasn't dominating or self-pleasing. It was with self-control and focused on the gratification he would receive at the end. His pleasure came directly from the pleasure he gave her. Every time Jovi responded with a sigh or a catch in her breath, Steele was motivated even more.

Jovi had had good sex before, but this was something else entirely. She had no reservations about what he thought of her naked, no second thoughts about he what would think about her vocal release of her pleasure. It was obvious from his body language that he wanted everything from her, and he wanted it raw and unfiltered.

They both lost their last clothing barrier that they had left, and Jovi's heart rate went through the roof. There was nothing more terrifying than the first time with a new man inside you. Even if it was something you wanted. Although every man was generally the same size, length, and width every measly centimeter made a huge difference in how her experience would be. "I'm nervous." She told him continuing her blunt and bold theme.

"Did you change your mind?" Steele asked. He carefully hesitated.

"No. That doesn't make me not nervous though."

"I'll be careful." He whispered.

Pain and pleasure mixed like a dance growing inside her. True to his word and his previous pace, he was methodical and gentle. He paid close attention to her reactions. It was clear when the pain had subsided, and desire was the strongest emotion. Even though it was becoming more and more difficult for Steele to hold himself back, he still kept his focus on Jovi. Her reaching her pleasure peak remained his target. When Jovi orgasmed, she was joined by Steele's within seconds as well. "Wow." Was all she could say.

Steele looked at her with hungry eyes and said. "I'm not done." He kissed her with even more passion and strength than he had yet. "But first, food."

Steele snuck down to the kitchen and grabbed a snack from the fridge. He came back into her room armed with cookies and milk. He munched down the cookies as he lounged on her bed. When finished, he put down the dishes and grabbed Jovi. "How do you feel about round two?" He whispered as he nibbled on her ear.

Hours later, Steele finally fell asleep. Round two and round three had all been totally different love making experiences. She couldn't believe the level of depth and sides Steele possessed. There was certainly spark and compatibility in the bedroom, but opening pandora's box just fueled her want for him more. Tonight though, Jovi felt glutinously sated. She didn't know what she had done to get so lucky, but she thanked the universe that this is where she was. She drifted off.

Chapter 14

They were awoken by a giant shattering noise. Steele jumped out of bed and put his arms on Jovi to keep her back. "What was that?" She asked. They flipped on the lights and looked around. Neither of them saw anything. Jovi bounded out of bed and grabbed her robe that was hanging from her door. Steele slid his jeans up and buttoned them hastily. Duchess was barking wildly while they dressed. She bounded down the stairs as they opened the bedroom door. Steele followed with Jovi dashing behind him. Jovi flipped on lights and Steele looking around every corner. When they reached the bottom of the stairs, Jovi felt a cool breeze and looked out her window. The window was shattered, and glass was lying everywhere. Tears flooded her eyes. Steele held her close. They would need to call the police, again.

"It's ok, beautiful. Just take a breath." Steele said. He called 911 dispatch. He explained the situation, and they told him they would send an officer out. "Jovi." He turned and looked at her. "It's been a long night. I know you are tired. There aren't enough officers available to help with something like this on a holiday. So, it's going to take longer than when Nick came. Get dressed and pack a bag for you and for Duchess. You guys are coming home with me when they are done. We can go pick up some security cameras in the city tomorrow, and I'll install them myself.

We can't wait for the ones that are coming anymore, and I don't think it's safe to stay here without them."

Jovi nodded. She was so frustrated and exhausted; she wasn't going to argue. *Who would want to frighten her so badly? Was it Nancy?* She had seen her with Steele at the carnival and had glared sternly at her when she left. Had it been Nick? He might have seen her as well and gotten angry that she was there with Steele and not with him. *Was it someone else entirely?* She wasn't sure she was any closer to having an answer. "Hannah is expecting me in the morning." That was all her mind could muster as she stared off into the night out of the window that was no more.

Steele grabbed her gently and spoke softly. "We will figure this out. I promise."

Jovi went upstairs, wordlessly, to pack a bag. She packed for a few days and grabbed the things she would need for sweet Duchess as well. She grasped her favorite quilt and the book she was reading. She tossed in her shower supplies and her notebook for the orchard. She folded up Duchess' leash and slid it in the bag.

She didn't want to leave her home. She looked around her. She wanted to be settling in, not constantly running, and looking over her shoulder. She needed to do something, to fight back. Maybe some investigating of her own needed to be done. She hurried downstairs to wait with Steele. Steele took her bags and walked her things out to his truck. He had already packed Duchess's food and bowls and had them loaded in the truck bed. As he was coming back inside, the lights of a police car shone in the driveway. A woman stepped out.

"Hey Tori. Thanks for coming. I know Fourth of July isn't the best night to have stuff like this going on."

"Steele, hey there!" Tori replied. "Either way I'm paid to do the same job until the morning comes." She turned to look at Jovi. "Jovi, I'm so sorry for this repeated harassment. I work the night shift, and I've been able to make it out most nights to check everything out, with it being the Fourth of July, it hasn't slowed down enough for me to have the time. I feel terrible." She said.

"I didn't think I'd have problems tonight either. Everyone seemed to be enjoying themselves at the festivities, but I guess I'm not far down the road. Thank you for the checking in you have been doing. I ordered that alarm system Luke had suggested right away, but it's been delayed in the mail. Steele and I just discussed picking one up tomorrow in person."

Tori nodded. "I think that's for the best if you want to be able to stay here safely while we figure this out. I'm concerned that the attack was on the house tonight. It's closer to causing you damage on your person, and I don't like that. Any new problems with anyone?"

Jovi shook her head no. "I did see the woman I had run into at the farmers' market tonight. Hannah identified her to me as Nancy Webster."

Tori took notes. "Did you speak to her today?"

"No, but she spoke with Steele and saw us walking away."

"Did you see Nick today?"

"No. I haven't seen him at all since the restraining order was placed."

Tori examined the window. A big red brick had been thrown at the center and shattered it all over her living room. Steele had loaded Duchess in the truck, so she wouldn't step on any of the glass. The room felt empty without her in it.

Tori took pictures and walked around both outside and inside. About one hour later she circled back to Jovi in the kitchen. "Are you able to stay somewhere else tonight?"

"Yeah. I'm going back to Steele's."

"Good." Tori replied. "We will figure this out. Whoever is responsible has not engaged in behavior like this before, so it's been harder to solve. We are actively working on it though."

"I know, and you guys have been truly wonderful. It's just a lot." She smiled a sad tight smile.

Tori handed Jovi her card. "I know you have Luke's number and that he is a close friend, but if you ever need something on the night shift, just call me."

Jovi smiled. She liked Tori. She had been kind and done her job well. It was nice to have a face to the officer that had been checking in on her. Jovi walked Tori to the door and went back to meet Steele. She found him wrangling her vacuum cleaner in the storage closet. "What are you doing?" She called to him.

"Cleaning." He said, not looking up from his task at hand. He proceeded to bring the vacuum to the living room and vacuum up as many of the little glass shards he could muster. He very carefully grabbed the large pieces and put them into a trash bag. He immediately took all the trash outside to her garbage bin. He took some measurements of the window and hung a blanket up in front of the hole. Jovi watched him as he went through his motions from the green couch. Her brain just could not connect what he was doing and why it needed to be done.

She began to feel cold and started to shiver. "Jovi, let's go." Steele said gently and guided her out to his truck.

Jovi climbed onto the front bench seat and looked out the window. Duchess placed her paws in her lap. Steele grabbed her hand and held it the entire ride. "Listen," Steele said. "I didn't know I was going to have company tonight." He explained.

"Steele, I don't have any expectations about the state of your house, I promise." She said grinning weakly.

"I know, but I wasn't' kidding when I told you my grandma would expect a man to keep a house just as well as the best woman can."

"Any man who regards what their grandmother would think at 3:00 in the morning, is the best kind of man." She kissed his hand. "Just keeping me safe tonight is enough." She said softer.

Steele lived in a little two-bedroom craftsman style house on the east side of town just past his store. Although technically still in the city limits, it was as far to the east as it could be without becoming "out of town." It was quiet with few houses nearby and limited traffic. The house had a large backyard. Although Steele had not been expecting company tonight, the outside lights glowed and lit up everything around it. Looking at it from the road, the grass was well maintained, and a simple flower bed was in bloom in the front. It lacked perennials like Jovi's bed. These flowers had been planted intentionally by Steele. Jovi was impressed he did any type of flower gardening. She had been spoiled on her property with large established plants like lilacs and lavender. She also had many bulb type flowers and flowers that reseeded themselves yearly. All Jovi had to do was weed the bed, but Steele had chosen this configuration himself, and it was lovely. One large, towering oak tree stood in the front yard and from it hung a simple rope swing with a board bench. Shadows danced on the property from the large objects that were partially illuminated by the porch light. Jovi thought it looked quaint, like a picture book.

She grabbed Duchess as Steele carried the bags and led her up the walk. When he unlocked the door, the house smelled like Steele. She hadn't been aware that he had a smell, but it was such a familiar and comforting smell, like chocolate chip cookies baking. She smiled. His anxiousness about the state of his house was evident as he zoomed around straightening his pile of mail and running into the bathroom to put out fresh towels and wipe down the sink. Despite his nervousness, his house was very tidy. Sure, it looked disheveled like someone had ran out of it earlier that day, but besides a rinsed dish sitting in the sink, clothes that had been discarded outside of the laundry room, and a cup that sat from breakfast in the living room, it was clean.

After he emerged from his cleanup of the bathroom, he gave her a tour. Duchess had already claimed his bed as her own and was nowhere to be seen. He showed her the kitchen, the cozy living room, and the bathroom. She could see the matching towel set he had carefully draped on the towel bars. He continued his tour. "So, my bedroom is the first door on the left. If you want to sleep alone, the guest bedroom is made up as well."

Jovi shook her head. "Why would I want to sleep alone?"

Steele shrugged. "I don't want you to feel like I'm making choices for you. I know you are very independent and wouldn't appreciate that at all. I was surprised that you let me talk you into spending the night here and leaving your home."

She threw her arms around his neck and pressed her lips against his. "I belong in your bed." She replied through kisses. He led Jovi into his bedroom. He grabbed the big quilt and draped it over the right side of the bed. He was apparently a left side sleeper. Jovi crawled under the covers and pulled the quilt up over her shoulders. Duchess stood up and adjusted her curl by her legs. She was already sleeping when Steele crawled in next to her and pulled her close.

Steele's room had black out curtains hung from both windows. At her own home, Jovi was used to waking up with the sun, but after the late night they had had, she was grateful the room had total darkness. When Jovi finally opened her eyes, Steele was gone from his side of the bed and Duchess was not in her usual spot. Jovi got up and went to the bathroom. When she emerged, she still didn't see or hear Steele and Duchess. She walked out to the kitchen and saw a note on the counter.

Jovi,

The store puts on a float for the parade today that I am expected to be there for. I'm sorry I couldn't miss it, but I know you are safe at my house. I took Duchess with. The kids will love her, and you can try to relax for a bit. I called Hannah to let her know you were at my place. She is picking you up at 11:30. She said something about having the works. We can meet back at my place after. I left you a key. The store that sells the alarm systems isn't open today because of the Fourth, so we can go first thing in the morning.

Steele

Jovi glanced at the clock, she had thirty minutes until Hannah would be there. Her stomach roared in protest of missing breakfast, but if Hannah had "the works" and knew how horrid her night had been, she would be soon absolutely stuffed. So, she ignored the hunger pains and jumped in the shower. She was dressed within ten minutes and decided to take a look at Steele's house in the daylight. His bedroom was painted an inviting shade of green. The bed had no throw pillows, but the bedding was a tasteful flannel with shades of green that crossed throughout the brown color and had a stitched texture. A picture of his parents on their wedding day hung on the wall in the hallway. They looked so in love just like Steele had described. He looked a lot like his mom with his father's strong frame. A baby picture of his nephew was nearby. The living room was tidy. A dark black shaggy rug lay on the floor in the middle. The leather chair that he clearly sat in daily had an end table against it. On the table was a book that sat facedown open to the page he was on. *Steele was a reader?* She had noticed him examining her bookshelf at home, but they hadn't yet discussed reading. Jovi had never met a man that read in his leisure time before and was used to that not being a part of conversation in her dating life. She took a closer look to see what he was reading. *Call of the Wild* by Jack London. Jovi's heart fluttered. They liked reading the same types of books. Jovi was an avid reader and was excited for nights that they could spend on her green couch quietly reading. She hated all the events and the constant "going out" she had been forced into in the city. Having a man who matched her own quiet pace and having him excite her to the core, just felt like a dream.

She wandered back into the kitchen. Although it was spotless and without clutter, two well used cookbooks sat near the stove. He owned more spices than just salt, pepper, and garlic. He must be able to cook then. His current life contained family, running the store, fishing, and dating her, so he probably had been eating out more than what he was used to. She looked forward to having a homecooked meal for dinner tonight. She had completely gorged herself with deep fried foods the entire day yesterday, and she knew this morning would be filled with Hannah's breakfast desserts. She definitely needed to eat something that contained some nutrients for dinner. Thinking about food made her stomach growl even louder.

The doorbell rang. Jovi immediately looked for Duchess, and then remembered she had gone with Steele. She was glad Hannah was here because being completely alone after the night she had had was jolting her. She opened the door for Hannah. Hannah immediately hugged her. She pulled her away by the shoulders and looked at her. "Are you ok?" Hannah searched her face for the truth.

"I'm not sure." Jovi replied. "I'm not physically hurt in any way, but I'm tired of the attacks on my home. I want them to find the culprit. I've had enough."

Hannah nodded. "I understand. You know Luke, Steele, and I will do everything we can do help."

Jovi smiled. "I know you will. I just don't want to get behind at the orchard, and I don't want to live in fear." She said.

"We can come up with a plan later over Ben & Jerry's." Hannah smiled at her. "In the meantime, let us parade. At the very least we will show the town that you aren't rattled, even if you are just a bit." She linked arms with Jovi, and they walked to her Bug.

"I have fresh coffee, doughnuts of three different varieties, and strawberry turnovers at Drury Lane. Marg has it open this morning for the parade traffic. I hid enough for us in the back." Hannah said. Hannah was like an energizer bunny.

How had Hannah done all that today with how late the night had been last night? Jovi couldn't wait to sit down with a doughnut and some hot coffee. The drive to the bakery was less than five minutes. They pulled the Bug into the alleyway behind the bakery and went in through the back. Hannah had gone and gotten coffee from the only coffee shop in town, Woods and Brews, and the largest size lattes that they sold sat on top of the counter next to enough food for five people. They grabbed their coffees and each of them filled up a paper plate with warm yeasted treats. Jovi grabbed two strawberry turnovers and balanced them on top. They sat on the sidewalk in front of the bakery in the chairs that Hannah had placed for them earlier. Jovi took a sip of the latte that was still hot. Even though it was July, and the weather was sweltering, Jovi had not been able to actually feel warm since last night. She took a huge bit of the doughnut. It was heavenly.

Hannah greeted her customers that entered Drury Lane, and they ate until they couldn't eat another bite. The parade was finally starting, and Marg had closed the bakery until after it was finished. She went to sit with her family and threw Hannah a smile. Jovi and Hannah were finally alone, well as alone as they could be in a crowd. "So," Hannah said. "Tell me about last night."

Jovi started with arriving home and the sex with Steele. "It was incredible. I have been with too many men who rush it through and in the end only care about their own ending. Much like the relationships I've been in. This was something else though. It felt like he wanted to know everything about me and how my body works. I've never felt so beautiful."

"The chemistry was obviously there in the bedroom then." Hannah winked.

Jovi nodded. "It really was. Best sex I've had." She chuckled and blushed. She finished her story with the damaged window and ending up at Steele's.

Hannah listened intently nodding along. "Jovi, I think that even after you install those security cameras, you shouldn't stay there alone until we catch whoever is doing this. Steele and I can switch off staying over, or you can stay at either of our places. I know you want to keep working on the orchard though, so we can make sure someone is there." "My mom is coming Friday." Jovi said. "We can figure it out. One day at a time." Hannah said as she grabbed her hands. "You aren't in this alone."

Chapter 15

They watched the parade with the marching band in the lead. Jovi searched for Steele's float as they passed by. The kids ran from all over the place at the candy being thrown into the streets. Finally, she saw Duchess come into focus. She was walking with Steele who was handing out icies to the kids. Her tail wagged as the kids petted and occasionally shared their treat with her. She looked at his float, which was an oversized looking toolbox decorated with American flags and saw the toolbox had an older couple seated together smiling widely and waving. On another set of chairs a little boy sat on his mother's lap. Her face looked identical to Steele's with a softer look. A man sat at her side. There were other people walking along the float with Steele. Jovi recognized one of the cashiers.

Jovi looked back. Steele caught her eye and his entire face lit up. He finished handing out the icies to the swarm around him and walked up the Jovi, wrapped his arm around the back of her head, and simply placed a giant kiss on her lips. There was a cheer that had gone out over the crowd. Jovi's cheeks burned red when he released her. Duchess decided that she had had enough of the marching and sat down at Jovi's feet. Steele handed her the leash, and he continued down the street to the next hoard of kids. Hannah stared at her with her mouth wide open. Jovi glanced back at the float to see the woman who looked like Steele give her a curious look and a knowing smirk. The older couple too studied her. "Did Steele just lip lock you in front of his entire family, and the whole town?" Jovi couldn't speak but sat there with a huge smile. "Well, someone else is tired of you being threatened as well. Talk about taking a stand." They laughed uncontrollably.

After the parade, Jovi was ready to lay low. The weekend had been incredibly long, and tomorrow would be even longer with fixing the damage at Autumn Gold and traveling for the security cameras. Jovi yawned. Hannah had gone into the shop to run the register for the second half of the day. Jovi took the walk down Main Street with Duchess to pick up her Subaru and drive it back to Steele's. She squeezed through people making their way to the amphitheater for the afternoon concert. Jovi glanced across the street and caught a glimpse of Nick. He locked eyes with her and shot her an icy glare. She held his gaze searching in his face for any signs that he was the one responsible for trying to destroy Autumn Gold. He dropped her eye contact and walked the other direction. Jovi shivered again. She picked up her pace and continued the walk to retrieve her car.

Vehicles were just starting to be let through the downtown, and she had to wait in line to drive through the parade route. This was the first time she had experienced traffic in this town, and it made her laugh out loud to herself. It took longer to find her car and get through the downtown traffic than it would have taken her to walk straight to Steele's, but she couldn't leave her car there any longer. She also wasn't exactly in a hurry. Steele hadn't said in his note when he would be back home after the parade. After watching Hannah be bombarded with customers, she thought that Steele may be stuck in the same boat. Not to mention, his family probably had a few questions for him as well.

When she arrived at Steele's, Steele wasn't there. Jovi wasn't surprised but being at Steele's house without him made her miss Autumn Gold, her own home. She decided to drive out there and check on the place briefly in the daylight.

When she arrived, she was relieved to find she didn't have any new damage. The window in the living room would be replaced tomorrow and the security cameras would be installed. She spent some time watering her garden and checked on the trees. Satisfied, she said good-bye to her home. There was a lot of work to do and Jovi hoped that this would be the last time she was forced to put it off for another time. As she drove away, she saw tire tracks on a small access road that didn't go anywhere. The tire tracks led behind a tree; you wouldn't be able to spot a vehicle here from the road. Jovi glanced towards her house. She wouldn't hear them leaving either, but Duchess would. She would let Tori know about this place so she could keep an eye out when she came over on patrol. She drove back to Steele's house. She was a bit surprise to see he still hadn't arrived, but Duchess and Jovi unlocked the door with her spare key and went inside.

Getting away from the crowds and the heat of the day made Jovi realize how tired she was. She took Duchess back into the bedroom and promptly fell asleep. When she awoke, Jovi was disoriented. *Where was she? What was that smell?* She looked around and remembered she was at Steele's. She must have slept for longer than she had intended. Jovi glanced at her watch, 5:00 PM. She had slept the entire afternoon away. Jovi inhaled again. It smelled like something was being pan fried. Jovi walked to the bathroom to fix her tousled hair and quickly brushed her teeth before she headed into the kitchen.

Steele was quietly chopping vegetables and frying them in his wok. Two pieces of salmon sat thawed on the counter dressed in lemon pepper and butter and laced with lemons. The smell was delicious, and Jovi was once again starving. "Hi handsome." She called from the hallway as he looked over and smiled.

"I didn't want to wake you. You were out hard when I got here. Duchess barely moved besides a sad tail wag to say hello."

Jovi smiled. This man was always thinking about her needs. "This is impressive." She gestured to the dinner. "I didn't know you cooked."

He nodded. "As an expert single man for many years, I made it a point to learn to cook. I got tired of take out after growing up with my mom making every meal, there is no comparison. She started shooing me away from eating there every night as well."

Jovi laughed. "I agree. I like to cook too. My grandma taught me. I always enjoyed pouring over her handwritten recipe books with her creating the most delicious magic. My mom isn't much of a cook. We had a lot of cheap take out growing up. Now she is married to a man that can cook the best food. I also am mostly sick of take out for life. I only like to go out to eat if it's something I'm not likely to make at home. Like sushi, or Thai. How was the parade?"

He nodded. "My grandmother was an excellent cook and so is my mom. I wish I would have sat down with her and begged her to teach me. I was content just eating it. The parade was good. The icies made it most of the way.

They are always a huge hit. My dad loves to ride the float and was thrilled at the amount of people that came up to catch up with him. That probably took more time than the parade itself, but I love to see him back in his element. I had to help take him home at the end and that took a little bit too. My sister asked me who the stunning woman I was kissing public was, and then my mom insisted you come to dinner next week. Half of my customer base congratulated me, and then I came home." He continued chopping like he had made a comment about the weather.

"Umm excuse me?" Jovi said. Steele looked up with a grin on his face. "Your mother invited me to dinner?"

"That's correct." He answered. Then he put the salmon in the oven and turned behind him to finish the baby red potatoes as he sprinkled them with herbs and drizzled oil, and he popped them in with the salmon. He came around the kitchen island and sat down by her and grabbed her hands. "I'm meeting your mother this weekend, and that was okay with you?"

Jovi nodded. "I think it's ok for you to meet my parents also." Jovi swallowed hard.

"Are you having doubts about being with me? Was last night disappointing? I can't say I'm the most experienced in bed, but I thought we were firing on the same cylinders."

Jovi looked at him. "Last night was amazing. No regrets and no comparisons." She kissed his cheek slowly and lightly. "Meeting the parents is just another big step, another big step that is totally new to me."

"I understand, but you are such a likeable person, Jovi. They are going to love you. Just like I do." He said slowly and raised his face to hers.

Her mouth dropped wide open. "Are you trying to give me a heart attack tonight?"

"All the vandalism and the threats against you just made me wild, and I'm known for keeping a level head. The only thing I want to do is keep you safe. The way Nancy and Stacey treated me yesterday like I couldn't possibly think of being with someone else made me irate. Hearing that Nancy talked to you like you didn't have any business thinking you could run a business or be with me, I've just had enough of it. I was trying to go slow, so I didn't spook you, but it's the truth. I love your tenacity and love for your orchard. I love how you make people feel like they are the most important and only thing in the room worth hearing when they talk to you. I love your judge of character and how the people you befriend become like family to you. I love how much you love historical items and traditions. I love your dog. I love your bookshelves that is overflowing with books, some of which I've actually read myself. I love that we can have intelligent conversations with each other. I love that you have a tenderness to you that comes out when you are worried you have overstepped someone. I think you are the most beautiful woman I've ever met, and I can't believe you would want to be with someone as non-exciting as I am. "

Jovi felt like the room was spinning and her eyes were seeing spots. *He loved her? He had noticed all those things about her and had decided he loved her?*

He rubbed her hands together to bring her focus back to him. "I haven't really dated because I was tired of being with a woman who didn't match me like a partner. I didn't want to be treated like a symbol. The other woman around me were the same. I was sick of the women who were pretty but possessed no substance and whose personalities were as fake as the layers of makeup they wear. I've been waiting for a partner, Jovi, and an equal. Someone I can hand anything in the world off to and vice versa. Someone to be an extension of myself. Someone who I can have long conversations with because God knows that's the glue that holds my parents together after all these years. Someone who I can sit with by the water with and have them watch the waves and see the beauty as I do while I fish, without complaining about being outside or just filling the space with noise."

Jovi had listened to all his reasons and realized most were things she had been noticing herself about him. *Maybe he wasn't wrong to love her, but did she love him too?*

"I'm not expecting you to say it back tonight. I just wanted you to accept it without denying it. I know that takes a bit to swallow. But just think about how David loves your mom. I know you didn't grow up watching her in love, but looking at her now, you know love is real. Right?"

She nodded. David worshipped her mom, and she knew it. She had watched Charlie and Caroline and knew they were in love. They had an equal partnership. Hannah and Luke and the way they just seemed better versions of themselves together, she knew that they were in love. Love was real, and it was all around her. So, could she accept that Steele might love her in the same way? "Ok." She whispered.

He kissed her and said softly. "I can show you in another way if you can't understand it in words." They entered his bedroom and closed the door.

Chapter 16

Jovi thought that salmon was the best she had ever had. She was so grateful to have something to eat besides funnel cakes and cotton candy tonight. "Oh my gosh Steele. I can't believe you didn't lead with 'by the way I can cook.' This is the way to have a killer first date and nail it. It would have won me over immediately.'" She almost audibly moaned through every bite. The baby potatoes just melted in her mouth and the vegetables were clearly fresh right out of someone's garden.

"So, tomorrow, we can go to the city in the morning. I talked to the guy who can do your window replacement today. I didn't mean to overstep, but he came up to me to tell me about his fishing trip to Canada so I figured I would take advantage that I had his ear. I gave him the dimensions. He is going to come over tomorrow and work on it while we grab the cameras. I'll get the cameras installed and working. Then you will have to decide where you want to stay or who you want to stay with you."

"Hannah said she could stay with me, too. Do you have plans tomorrow night?"

He shook his head. "I will need to spend some time at the store tomorrow, but I am pretty flexible as to when I get that done."

"Why don't you work on that after the security cameras are installed? We can trial them out while you are working. I'll catch up on the orchard, and then I can make you dinner." She said.

He nodded. "That's probably a good idea. If anything went wrong, I can be there quickly. It will only be a few hours. I can do that."

"Do you mind if we make a few other stops tomorrow? I need a few things for my mini bakery and for my mom coming up."

"Of course." He answered. "When is she coming?"

"Friday morning." Jovi replied. "I don't know if I want you guys there every night while she is visiting."

"I understand that. I'll at least not have plans in the evenings she is here, just in case."

They continued the meal with lighter conversation. Jovi asked him about his favorite books. He asked her about her favorite meal. They asked about favorite vacations and music. Jovi was grateful for easy conversation without having to discuss love and the violence on her farm. For just a minute it felt like everything was right in the world. It seemed like any topic that wasn't talked about prior they thoroughly chewed over tonight. They had the same taste in music and movies. They had similar favorite novels. Jovi couldn't believe how much it seemed this man had been molded to be hers. They complimented each other in the best way.

After dinner, they cleared the dishes together. He washed. She dried. Then, they settled in the living room. Steele sat in the worn leather chair and picked up the *Call of the Wild.* Jovi pulled out her orchard book and started planning what she would need to do this month. She needed to get the word out about some temporary part time hires for the season. Jovi also wanted to build an area to put some already harvested pumpkins. Jovi thought of the crowds she would be attracting. She would have families with children and young people who wanted the fall experience complete with fall pictures. *What could she add that catered to those groups?* She was happy with her product. The pre-picked and pick your own option plus the baked goods, covered most of what customers would want, but she hadn't done much planning about the experience. She mentally walked around her property. She thought it was crawling with magic and in the fall, it would be completely aglow. She needed to have that magic easily accessible. Maybe Steele could create a metal creation with Autumn Gold branding that kids and couples could take pictures by. She glanced up at him.

He immediately caught her eye and grinned. Jovi already had the hayride planned which she was pretty certain would be popular, but what about a walking path that took them through the woods and back? Something simple and short, but that gave the customers that wanted to explore more, a taste of how the glow of the leaves made the woods feel like fairies and elves lived behind every corner. She knew her property well enough to know exactly where she wanted to have it placed. She could do a glow hike for opening night along with a bonfire.

It felt good to finally be focused on her vision again. She started to feel cooped up sitting at Steele's and restless. As if on cue, Steele placed his book face down, just as Jovi had found it early, stood up and came to sit down next to her. "What are you working on? Can I see?" He asked.

Jovi explained her vision and asked about a photo area. "That's really clever." He said smiling at her. "Those photo areas usually are wooden with gaudy colors. This is something unique. You could add some of the flowers that you are growing, some pumpkins. Add color that isn't tacky to give it something extra."

Jovi looked surprised. "You are really good at this."

He shrugged.

"So, can you make me something?"

"Absolutely. What else do you have here?"

She showed him the area she had cleared for the hayrides. "But I also want to do another walking path to showcase the orchard and then the woods. I figured I could add a lighted option on a few special nights of the season, opening night for starters. I also want to hang some lights and do an area for a bonfire."

"Jovi, people will really like this."

Jovi smiled. She thought so too.

The next morning, Jovi began to get a feel for what day to day life could be like with Steele in it. She woke up with the sun, even though the curtains blocked it out. She took Duchess on a run around town. It was a perfect morning void of humidity, but full of sunshine and friendly faces. When they got back to Steele's, he had the coffee pot running and was scrambling eggs in the kitchen. "How do you like yours?" He said looking up. "Eggs are one thing that people are usually particular about."

She smiled. "I'll have them how you are having them." After she stretched and showered, he placed a plate of scrambled eggs with peppers and mushrooms topped with feta cheese and bits of bacon on the kitchen island. She grabbed a mug that had a picture of a walleye on it and filled it to the brim with coffee and creamer. He sat in the stool next to her with his identical plate of eggs and his second cup of coffee. Her cheeks burned as she thought of how much she would like this scene to replay for the next 70 years.

It gave her anxiety to think of how much she was getting attached to Steele. Getting attached would mean not leaving, and that would mean negotiating conflicts that might not benefit her. She wasn't great at compromise, and had a hard time trusting others to make decisions that affected her. She drank her coffee and tried to realign her thoughts and relax. Steele had assertively helped her fix the damage on her orchard and kept her safe. He had made decisions without her, but good ones, and never had he been aggressive or controlling, just helpful. Jovi reminded herself that trust was a component of having someone be an extension of yourself, and that even the daughter of a single mom was capable of it. *What was it that Caroline had said? That Lynn had limited herself to the happiness she thought she deserved.* Jovi was not going to make that same mistake.

Before they left to go to the city, Jovi called Mario, the man who would be replacing her window. He verified that he would be coming today and the cost. Jovi hoped there weren't be too many more problems like this. She had budgeted for farm equipment and orchard investments, but she didn't have unlimited funds available to damage caused by someone who just didn't like her. She sighed and thanked Mario. She assured him she would be seeing him later and hung up.

Jovi didn't want Duchess to be roaming around Steele's entire home unsupervised, and it was too hot to have her in the truck all day long, so she got her settled in his bedroom. She seemed to like that best. She also seemed to be very tired out from the marching that Steele had made her do the day before. She didn't protest in the least and was sleeping before Jovi shut the front door.

The drive to the city was a few hours and Jovi and Steele filled the time with conversation about opening day, fishing, and when Steele would be coaching again. He coached hockey, which was a winter sport, but he was the volunteer that ran open ice. They put this on a few times during the summer and encouraged the team to come and skate along with the public. "Do you skate?" He asked her.

"A little. It's been years though. I never was a hockey player or in ice skating so I can't say that I am that good."

"That doesn't matter." He said grinning at her. "There is an open skate in August. I want you to come with me. You should get comfortable with the rink for the winter. I spend a lot of time there."

He was thinking into the future too. Jovi smiled at the thought. "Alright, I'll give it a try."

They spent some time in silence then, listening to the radio and feeling the wind blow into the truck. Steele held her hand gently as they finished the drive to the Best Buy.

Since they had the exact product that Jovi had ordered online through another company, they quickly bought the cameras and headed out the door. Efficient, just like Steele seemed to like. He got things completed and then spent time in reflection mode. It was a rhythm that Jovi understand and recognized in herself. "That was quick." She remarked. Can we make another stop?"

He nodded. "You said you needed a few things for your mom visiting. Show me the way." They laughed as he did a robot impersonation. It wasn't often he was goofy, and he certainly didn't like to be the center of attention like

Luke did, but he was playfully, funny and Jovi really liked that.

Jovi went into the Bed Bath and Beyond and bought some sheets for her spare bedroom. It had come with a complete set, but Jovi didn't know how old it was. She picked up a fan for the spare bedroom. She was lucky enough to have central air, but sometimes the upstairs got a tad stuffy, with her mom being pregnant, she wanted to ensure she got a good night sleep. Hannah was planning on spending some nights over as well, and it was important to Jovi that she was also comfortable and not dreading those nights.

She bought a few mixing bowls, measuring cups, spatulas, Bundt cake pans, and cookie sheets. Jovi didn't have a collection large enough to bake on the scale that she planned on. She wanted to be able to use both ovens as well as Lynn did. That would require many more pans than what she currently owned. She ended the trip with new towels. Hers were looking ragged, and she was embarrassed thinking about her guests using them. She didn't need anything fancy, but she wanted towels that didn't look like a rat had chewed them up.

Despite going through most of the store, she made her decisions quickly, and Steele didn't fuss about being along on a shopping trip or her wasting too much time. He pushed the cart and answered any questions Jovi gave him about sizes or colors. He even grabbed a new throw blanket for himself. It felt good to have a man with he didn't think shopping with her was silly and reminding of her exactly of that every few minutes. When they checked out, Jovi knew it was lunch time before even looking at her watch.

"So, show me your favorite spot to eat here." Steele said. "I can't say I did any preparing on where we would go for lunch. You know the city better than I do. "

Jovi gave him directions to her favorite Italian place. They ordered their food to go and went to the park to eat at the picnic tables that sat out year-round.

"How does it feel being back here?" Steele asked. "Do you miss it?"

Jovi looked around her before responding. "I feel like that was a hundred years ago. I don't miss anything about this place. I feel like I have changed ten-fold since moving to Woodsburrow. I would never be able to move back here and feel like I belonged. That is a feeling I have only gotten since moving." She grinned thinking about the first time she laid eyes on Autumn Gold. That home feeling that continued to ground her was making her feel stronger, and more of herself. She looked at Steele. He had a frown on his face and was running his hand through his hair. *Was he worried she was happier being here?*

"What's wrong?" She asked.

"I just feel like there is an entire side of you I never knew. That I won't ever know. What if that urge comes back? To be in the city and being achieving big things and touching all the action? What if Woodsburrow is too small and dull for you? What if being with me is too boring for you?"

She shook her head. "I never liked living here. And I moved here because I thought I was supposed to. That sounds stupid saying that out loud. I always hated the noise and lights and the traffic. There isn't one second since I moved that I think about being back. I didn't leave friends or family here. This chapter in my life is just complete. I don't feel any temptation." She grabbed his hand. "Now with you on the other hand, my strongest emotion might be temptation."

He grinned. "If only my truck had enough space to explore that." He nibbled on her fingers. "There's always tonight." He shot her a wink.

Chapter 17

When they returned to Woodsburrow, Steele and Jovi were in business mode. They picked up Duchess, who greeted them like they had been gone for years and not a morning, and Jovi's Subaru, and they went straight to the orchard. Mario was just finished up the windowpane, and it looked fantastic. She had opted for a glass that was supposed to insulate the house better, and she could see the thickness difference was obvious to what she had previously had. "Thank you so much, Mario. You did a fantastic job."

Mario didn't say much but she could tell he was pleased with the job he had done and Jovi's reaction. She paid him, and he left. Meanwhile, Steele had gotten a giant head start at installing the security cameras. In fact, he was almost done. He planned on running into town to do his work at the store after.

Jovi finished unloading Steele's truck of her shopping bags and overnight bags and read the instructions on how to connect with the cameras. She had completed the hook up from her phone easily and could see all the camera views from the living room. She kissed Steele goodbye, and although she could tell he was nervous to leave her there, he left without protesting.

The afternoon had started to fade, and Jovi was grateful to be home. The silence of the walls around her after an exciting event was one of her favorite feelings. It gave her the time to reflect on her experiences and soak in her gratitude. She sat quietly in her living room with her new living room window sparkling in the sunshine.

What was next? She wondered. She had a big week in front of her, a big couple months in fact. It was vital she get ready on time and that people felt safe to visit her orchard. She hadn't seen her home for more than a few minutes since Thursday. Anything that was alive and growing was in an unruly state and would need mowing, weed pulling or harvesting. The baby trees she had planted needed to be watered. She had to start cleaning the house for her mother's visit. She wanted her to feel welcome and comfortable while she stayed. She would have Steele and Hannah in and out and she felt like she was being pulled in a million directions. She could feel the tightness and overwhelm building in her chest and her frustration grew towards the culprit. The extra work that the vandal had created was enough to give her anxiety. She took a long breath. *One thing at a time.* She told herself. This was her dream, and no one was going to take that from her.

Jovi went upstairs and changed into her orchard working clothes. One thing at a time. That was how she could tackle this. She left Duchess on the couch taking her nap and went outside to mow the lawn. It was a very meditative experience and when she finished, the tightness in her chest had begun to release. She could breathe again. Duchess had her face pressed up against the glass, her tiny nose creating little figures on the window when she breathed out, so Jovi let her out so she could join her. She knelt down in the flower bed and pulled the weeds as she enjoyed the full bloom of the roses, peonies, lavender and holly hocks. The color was brilliant against the story book style exterior of her home. She could imagine Lynn planting these tenderly, years ago. Now, here she was enjoying magnificently large peonies and lavender so established she had never seen one so full. She loved touching something alive in the dirt. It made her feel like she was helping preserve a little piece of history. She for years had run past the women in the elaborate historical houses in the city as they spent early mornings in the flower beds. She had often wondered if they did that for pleasure or to keep up with the Jones. She knew the answer now.

She watched as Duchess had ran her "zoomies" around the yard and settled down under the shade of her giant trees with a chosen stick. She couldn't remember what she had spent her afternoons doing in the city. Her life had been so empty. She reflected. She hadn't understood what she needed or what life was about at all. Now, she understood that her life needed community, the dirt, the forest, her kitchen, friendship, books, music, art, and love. All of those things were important. They were the spices that turned something as dull as egg cooked in water to something coveted like eggs benedict.

Duchess and Jovi went inside as her stomach started to growl. She could have spent all night out there working, her body coming alive and mind drifting, but it was dinner time, and Steele would be coming back tonight. She started her laundry and made her bed with fresh sheets. She jumped in the shower and put on her favorite pair of sweatpants and a black t-shirt with a sunflower in the middle. She slipped on her cozy mustard yellow slippers and walked downstairs.

She had the feeling of a good day's work. She had been productive and was finally home. She was spending her evening how she wanted all of them spent. Jovi turned the porch light on so Steele would be able to see when he arrived. She lit candles downstairs; her favorite woodland scent filled the air. She vacuumed. There were still some glass shards on the ground they hadn't been able to see when it was dark. Satisfied, she went into the kitchen.

She had not had time to stop at the grocery store this week yet, but her garden was starting to give her a good harvest. She had garlic stipes, basil, beans, and kale and that was the basic ingredients for a vegetable pesto. She took out some chicken breast to marinate, and she fired up the grill. Kenny G's soothing saxophone rang out while she created the pesto, boiled pasta, and finally put the chicken on the grill. She had put together an impressive looking salad with the mixed greens and fresh herbs and drizzled leftover vinaigrette over the top. She hadn't heard from Steele yet, so she threw together a simple strawberry shortcake, with the strawberries the Grants had given her. She put the shortcake in the oven to bake while they ate dinner. The strawberry compote gently heated through on the stovetop.

She was so absorbed in her music when Steele walked up behind her and wrapped his arms around her in a huge hug, she jumped.

"I'm sorry. I wasn't particularly sneaky when I came in. Duchess came over to say hello. I couldn't help but watch you a minute swaying to the rhythm." He kissed her neck and she smiled. "It smells heavenly in here. You've been busy." He observed.

"Well, I did have a small pity party, but I think that helped me be more productive the rest of the day." She looked at him, still grinning. She felt like Duchess with her overwhelming amount of excitement every time she walked through the door, like it had been a hundred years instead of an hour since they had been together last.

"Everyone needs a pity party once in a while. I think you have done a great job holding it together, but if you don't let that out, it just builds inside you." He kissed her again, and then again.

She pushed him away while kissing him back. "No. Dinner." She said laughing.

They sat down and ate on the outside patio set she had added to the back porch. It had become her new favorite place to eat supper. The sun was starting to approach the horizon, although it wasn't setting just yet, it was dipping behind the woods and darkness started to slowly spread it fingers over the scenery around them. Having finished cooking, she had turned off the sweet melodies of Kenny G and the sounds of crickets were the only noise around them. An owl called out from the woods every couple of minutes. The tranquility that was present around her gave her the feeling that she would get through this chaotic time, the end was in sight.

"I don't want to have to run from my home anymore, Steele. I love this house, this land. It's where I am supposed to be."

He looked up at her. "I know, Jovi. The way you thrive here and come alive when you are working on this property, it gives you a color that you didn't have when we first met."

"Do you feel that same way about your house? Does it pull you in like that?"

He shook his head no. "I like it, don't get me wrong. It's a good house. It has a great yard. It's quiet. It suits my current needs perfectly. Long term though, I picture living in a space I can work on and maybe even fish on. My metalwork I need to do at my parent's right now because I don't have the right outside space for it. It's a very good house, but it's my for now house. I'm okay with that."

Jovi nodded. She understood. She pictured Steele in a house he could walk out to a creek with his fishing pole and leave his metal work where he currently was to go to the store but be able to come back to it unmoved and not feel like it was in someone's way. Her house suited her quirks and hobbies, it was different than just having four walls and good location.

When Jovi and Steele went upstairs for the night, they pulled up the security system to check what had been going on and to get familiar with how it functioned. The looked over the different cameras to see if anything had recorded on any of them. There was nothing but a few squirrels. She felt safer than she had in the past. Steele was there, her cameras were working, and Tori had texted her to let her know tonight was a night she would be driving by to check on her place. She made a mental note to make something to thank Tori for her kindness. Then, she drifted off to sleep, satisfied that it would be a good night.

The next day, Steele had to work. He was working the register for one of his employees, and he had to open the store. So, he was long gone before Jovi woke up. Jovi couldn't help but feel guilty how much time he had spent over the last few days helping her. She texted Steele to let him know Hannah would been spending the next few nights with her. That would give him some time to catch up on his own things. Then she sent Hannah a message. She was perky and positive even this early in the morning, but then, as a baker she was always up early. "I'll bring the popcorn!" She texted back.

Jovi and Duchess tried to spend as much time outside as they could in morning, before the heat of the day, and the next few days were supposed to be scorchers. They went out for a run, using the trails she had decided would be used in the fall to help pack it down. Then immediately Jovi went out into the garden. She harvested her ripe vegetables and weeded until she couldn't take it anymore and turned on her sprinklers. She came in for lunch and looked at her harvest basket. It looked like it would be chicken breast over a salad. The day was getting too hot to spend any more time working outside. Jovi spent the rest of the day in her air conditioning preparing the house for her mother's visit.

Hannah arrived for a late dinner. They chatted about the day. Jovi showed her the new alarm system, and she could tell that Hannah was relieved. They put on their pajamas, Jovi had a green set with white buttons down the front, and Hannah wore a matching pink set complete with pink fuzzy slippers. Jovi couldn't help but giggle. It was predictably Hannah.

"I found some boxes of Lynn's while I was cleaning today that have papers and old photos. Do you want to go through them with me?"

Hannah clapped her hands together. "Yes! Oh, that's exciting. Uncovering secrets from the past!"

They carried the boxes down to the living room. Duchess settled in, and they each grabbled a glass of wine.

Chapter 18

For the next few hours, they sifted through old newspaper clippings from Woodsburrow. Most were about Lynn or the orchard, some were about different events in town, marriages, and births, and some about the expansion of Richard Webster's empire. "I understand most of these clippings, and it's quite entertaining to read about the history of the town, but why the obsession with the Webster hotel chain?" Hannah asked.

Jovi shrugged. "I don't know. A lot of these are friends and neighbors, maybe Nancy was one of her friends from high school?" Jovi replied.

"Maybe." Hannah said. "I never saw them around together though. I didn't know her extremely well, but I did know that she was close with Caroline. It's weird I never saw her around with Nancy."

There were pictures of the orchard barn, all shiny and newly built. Pictures of harvest season and the visitors at the orchard. She had photographs from the Firelight Festival, and the Fourth of July. Pictures from a Christmas party she hosted yearly. The living room was packed with people. A huge tree stood in front of the large window adorned with lights. A large table was set up with cookies and appetizers. A delicate punch bowl sat at one end. It was an action shot; people were not posed. They were laughing and chatting and the overall feel in the room seemed joyous. It made Jovi feel glad to see Lynn in the company of so many people in the town that had made her feel like family as well. "You should bring this back!" Hannah exclaimed seeing the photograph she was holding.

Jovi nodded. "It looks like so much fun. I would love to host a tradition like this."

They moved on from the pictures to written letters. Some of the notebooks were journals about the orchard. Different trees and where they were located, different yields, and how the year had been. Jovi set those aside to read at her leisure. She wanted to see how busy Lynn had been, what the names of the tree varieties were and what had sold the best. They found Christmas cards and Happy Birthday cards. Jovi couldn't help but feel a wave of sadness. These were moments in Lynn's life that had been important to her, and there was no one left in the world who had wanted to own such treasures. At the very bottom of the box, there were some very thin and yellowing folded pages. Jovi carefully grabbed one and unfolded it.

My love,

These last few months with you have been incredible. You are such a beautiful woman and I long for the day we can walk down the street hand in hand together. When I am with you, I feel such joy. I admire you and the hard work and tenacity you have shown the in face of any, and all adversities you experience in building your orchard. I'll be free on Friday night at seven. Meet me at our spot.

King

"Oh my gosh!" Hannah and Jovi gasped together.

"It's a love note."

"I didn't know she had a lover!" Hannah squealed.

"I did, but I only know of the one. Caroline didn't know his name. Who is King?" Jovi asked.

Hannah shook her head. "I don't recognize that name. Are there any other letters?"

Jovi sifted through the pages and found another yellowing sheet.

My love,

I can't believe you are pregnant! As scared as I am, I look forward to being a father. I know our child will be as beautiful and as strong as you are. I'm going to tell my parents about us. You are the one I want to spend my life with. They will understand that we need to be a family.

King

"Pregnant?" Hannah squeaked. "I didn't know she had a child!"

Jovi shook her head. "She didn't. She lost the baby and whoever 'King' is never told his parents about their relationship. He married someone else."

"That's terrible. And sweet Miss Lynn never found love." Hannah said. Nothing else in the box was as exciting as the love notes.

The topic of love opened the discussion about Hannah's wedding plans. "So, did you decide on a date?" Jovi asked.

Hannah nodded. "February 14th of next year."

Jovi smiled. Hannah was such a romantic. "That is so sweet Hannah. You could do a theme with pink and hearts, a sweetheart romance. It suits you guys."

Hannah smiled. "I love the thought of having it in the winter. Will you be my maid of honor?" She said looking at Jovi.

"You are sure your sisters won't try to have me murdered in my sleep if I say yes?"

Hannah laughed. "No, they won't. I'm having them stand up as well, but I would say we are all quite different. It won't be a surprise to them that neither is maid of honor. It has the added benefit of them not arguing between each other either."

"I would be honored to be your maid of honor." Jovi and Hannah hugged. It had gotten extremely late. They finished their wine and headed to bed.

The rest of the week continued in the same fashion, by the time Friday morning came, Jovi could hardly contain her excitement at her mom's visit. When she pulled in the driveway at 10:00, she ran outside to say hello. "Mom!" She said as her mother got out of the car and held her. "You look amazing!" Jovi said looking her mom's precious belly. She did look amazing. She was glowing and looked like a goddess.

Her mother had always been stunning, and it seemed like as she aged, she just came into her beauty more and more. "You look radiant as well my beautiful daughter." She said kissing her cheek. "Love suits you." She teased and winked at Jovi. Jovi had gotten leaner since moving to the orchard. Her body was stronger and had more developed muscles. Her skin had color from her spent outside instead of pasty and pale from her office job. "You looked more relaxed and confident. It's the most beautiful thing I've ever seen." Her mother was always so boldly honest and spoke as though she was seeing her in one of her paintings.

Jovi blushed. "Thanks, Mom. Let me get your bags for you."

Jovi's mom had packed an overnight bag, a pregnancy pillow, her case of paints and a canvas. "Planning on doing some painting?" She asked as she brought her things inside.

She smiled. "You never know when the moment will strike you! Despite feeling swollen and slow, I still have my creativity."

"Are you feeling up for a tour?" Jovi asked. Jovi's mom nodded. "I'm feeling stiff from sitting. A bit of walking would do me good." Duchess was standing right inside the door and was wagging her tail so aggressively that Jovi thought her tail would wag right off. Her mother got down at her level and patted Duchess. She let her kiss her face, and she told her what a beautiful girl she was. "What a sweetheart, Jovi. Her soul obviously matches yours." She watched Duchess approach Jovi for another scratch between the ears.

Jovi started by showing her mother the inside of the house. She brought her to the bathroom and the upstairs bedrooms. She placed her mom's bags on the spare bedroom nearest the upstairs bathroom. Jovi had put a fan in the room and had put on the new sheets she had bought with Steele. She carefully placed the pregnancy pillow on the bed. After her mom emerged from the bathroom, Jovi brought her downstairs and showed her the living room. Her mother smiled seeing all of Jovi's book aligned around the fireplace. She was just as transfixed as Jovi was with the color palette inside her home and admired innate every detail. They went into the kitchen and headed out the door onto the back porch.

The view of the garden and the orchard was beautiful that morning. The sun was shining, and the birds were singing like it was a Disney movie. Her mother's breath caught. "Oh, Jovi. What an incredible view this is!"

"It's my favorite place to sit in the evening." She nodded.

"I can see why!" They continued their tour. Her mother marveled at her garden. "When did you learn how to garden?"

Jovi shrugged. "I don't know. When I moved in it just seemed like something I should do. So, I did it. It feels so natural. Caroline has taught me a lot, and there is so much more to learn, but I love it." She smiled at her mom.

"It suits you." She said happily back. Her mother inspected each one of her flowers. They walked towards the orchard barn and her mother saw her sign. "Wow Jovi. Where did you get that? It's very good. Did you draw it out for someone?" Jovi shook her head. "Steele made it for me. I told him what I was planning on calling the orchard, and he showed up with it."

Her mother looked at her. "Has he told you yet?"

"Told me what?" Jovi asked.

"That he loves you."

Jovi blushed furiously.

"And what did you say?" Her mother asked.

"I didn't say anything." Jovi answered.

"Because?" Her mom asked.

"I'm afraid." Jovi said. "I've never said that to a man before. It's a lot to give someone."

Her mom nodded. "It is. It is smart to think first, and not give that to everyone you meet. It's also wrong to not give your love when it's real. This man is showing you he loves you along with his words. That's powerful. Don't be afraid of love. I raised an independent, brilliant, and capable woman. It is okay to feel vulnerable sometimes too. Trying to avoid it, doesn't make you any less susceptible to unfortunate events. People in our lives make those mountains easier to climb."

Jovi nodded. "I've been noticing that. I am surrounded by people who have shown me so much kindness and support. I can't imagine doing any of the things I've done without them."

"I'm so proud of you and the growth you have gone through. You have transformed." They hugged.

Jovi brought her mother into the barn. She had set up most of the shop. Her vision needed little explanation. It was charming and easy to see how people would spend their time there in the fall. Jovi talked about the artisans who made each one of the items and the different stories she remembered. Her mother beamed with pride. "You have always had an artist's eye." She showed her the wall that had expanded and was now lined with photographs, newspapers clippings and the old items Lynn had own before. "What a beautiful way to pay tribute to this woman's life. I raised a good person." Her mom said with tears in her eyes as she kissed Jovi's head. They walked out to the orchard and walked down the rows of trees. Her mother examined the different apples growing and the character of the heritage trees as well as the impressive growth of her baby ones.

After their walk, they spent the rest of the day hanging out, just like old times. They laughed and caught up. Her mother had brought along ultrasound photos that they looked at together. The baby wiggled in her belly as they talked, and her mother laughed. For the first time since she heard about the pregnancy, she began to feel a connection to the baby and some excitement. She loved her little brother Silas, and this baby she would be able to help guide in life. She had time now with owning the orchard to spend more significant amounts of time visiting and maybe even watching them at her place, and she planned on using that time wisely. This was the time that her siblings would remember from their childhood and she wanted to give them a happy experience. She wanted to have a strong bond with them despite being much older.

"We aren't finding out the gender." Her mother announced. "It's very likely this will be my last pregnancy, and I'd like it be a surprise like you were."

"I like that." Jovi said grinning. "I'll be there when they are born. I can't wait to meet them."

They hugged.

She cooked her lasagna for dinner, and they ate on the porch enjoying the view. After dinner, her mother started to yawn. "Growing a baby at my age is no joke. Although, it's no joke at any age." She said stretching her arms into the air and rubbing her swollen belly. "I think I'm going to shower and go to bed."

Jovi nodded. "You look wiped. It's alright. I could use an evening of laying low anyway."

"I love you, my sweets. I'll see you in the morning." Her mother kissed her head and headed upstairs. Jovi settled on the couch with a blanket and a book.

Chapter 19

The next morning, Jovi had slept a bit later than normal. She looked around the room and didn't see Duchess, so she dressed for the day and headed downstairs. Her mother was already awake and was out on her porch with her canvas set up in front of her, brush in hand. Duchess ran around the backyard happily as she painted.

"Good morning Mom." She called from the kitchen. "Can I get you something? I'm going to make some coffee."

"A black tea if you have it."

"I'll be out in a few minutes." Jovi brewed a pot of coffee while her mom's black tea steeped. She entered the porch five minutes later drinks in hand. She set her mother's tea down next to her and settled in her favorite chair.

Jovi took a closer look at the picture her mother was painting. As soon as she saw it, she knew exactly what it was and looked out in front of her. It was a perfect replica of the view from her back porch. The flowers were in full bloom. The sun was rising up over the trees.

"Mom, it's my land!"

"It was too perfect not to paint it." Her mom smiled a lazy smile like she was in a daze.

Jovi watched her paint as she drank her coffee. It felt like she was a kid again making her magic come to life. Jovi made them both omelets and got a second cup of coffee. As she ate and sipped, the sun slowly rose in the sky and her mother's painting continued to transform.

When her mother finally stood up with her paint brushes to wash them off and use the bathroom, it was almost lunch time. The blank canvas had transformed into an identical copy of the scene around here. Her garden was on the left and looked luscious and enchanting. As she looked across the canvas, the middle portion captured her orchard barn with the Autumn Gold sign Steele had lovingly created for her. On the far-right side, up the rolling hills, was the orchard in all its magnificence. The sun was rising over the forest.

Tears rolled down her face. This was her favorite painting her mom had ever created.

Her mom emerged in the doorway rubbing her lower back. "That's the longest I've painted continuously in a while, but the bug hit me, and I just had to get it on paper."

"Mom, I love it!"

"Good sweetie. Hopefully, you have a place for it." She looked at the canvas and smiled in satisfied way.

Jovi smiled too. "Above my favorite couch. I'll have Steele hang it when he comes later."

"I'm meeting him? You've never let me meet a boyfriend before!" Her mom couldn't contain her excitement. "When is he coming?"

"This afternoon sometime. He had a hockey volunteer event this morning. He is the head coach and takes it pretty seriously." Jovi responded.

"Would you mind if I painted some pieces for your orchard barn display?" Her mom asked.

"I'd be honored. Mom, you don't have to do that. You have pieces in fancy art galleries all over the place."

"But having them here would mean the world to me."

She smiled. Jovi might have grown up without a dad, but her mom was the absolute best mom she could have ever hoped for.

Jovi took her mom on the hiking path she had cleared for the fall. They weaved through the orchard, went over the hill, and walked down into the woods. The trees were green and full, and the sun shone down in patches on the forest floor. They got to the turnaround site, which was a cleared circle in the woods.

"You should put a bench here." Her mom remarked. "What a perfect place to sit and enjoy before heading back."

It was the perfect place. A ring of birch trees surrounded the area in a perfect fairy ring. You could see the creek running just down the hill and hear it rushing by. They listened until they had their fill, and then walked back to the house.

When they reached the barn, they could see Steele arriving. He had a giant metal creation in the back of his truck. "Jovi!" He called. "I brought your photo backdrop. It's pretty heavy. Where do you want me to put it?"

"You made that already? We just talked about it Sunday."

He shrugged. "I knew exactly how it was supposed to look. So, I made it."

Her mother lit up like a candle. "He has an artist soul. I love him already." She said to Jovi and smiled.

"You can drive it back over here." Jovi called back and pointed to a spot behind the barn towards the orchard.

There was nothing there currently, but it was exactly in the area her customers would walk past. Steele backed his truck to the back of the barn and unloaded it carefully.

After he finally got it standing on the ground, he was huffing and puffing and sweat beads had formed on his forehead. Jovi walked to face it so she could see the piece. It was magnificent. The metal creation was seven feet tall. It was a giant apple tree. There were multiple apples around the border. Autumn Gold Orchard was worded in the center of the tree. The detailing was incredible. Jovi could see where she could place bushels of apples, pumpkins, and mums for photographs. It was perfect. "Steele." She whispered. She could see the tears in her mom's eyes. Jovi hugged Steele and whispered, "Thank you." "This is my mom. Mom this is Steele." Jovi said introducing them.

Her mom wiped the tears out of her eyes. "It's so nice to meet you. I've heard so much. I'm very impressed with your metalwork." They shook hands.

Steele ran his hand through his hair. "Thank you. I can't say that I'm an expert, but I really enjoy doing it. It's so good to meet you. You raised a phenomenal woman, and I've been looking forward to it. I brought lunch." He said and headed for his truck. He held up the two brown paper bags and led the walk to the house.

Jovi's mother turned and looked at her, "If you don't marry him. I might leave David for him. You've managed to hook an amazing catch." They giggled.

Steele had picked up Jovi's favorite pulled pork sandwiches with French fries. *Where had he drove for these?* They sat and ate as Jovi's mom and Steele got to know each other. Steele was friendly and kind. He held Jovi's hand occasionally and brushed his fingers across her palm. He seemed very at ease with her mother. Her mother was more than thrilled to meet someone that Jovi was dating. This had never happened before. They talked about art. Jovi was shocked at all the famous painters and artists Steele could speak to. This was more than the mere hobby he had made it look like it was. Art was a passion for him. He spoke about the store and his family. They talked about fishing and coaching. Her mom asked questions and actively listened for the answers. She watched closely as Jovi and Steele interacted. Jovi left the room to use to the bathroom and left them alone.

"She loves you; you know. I've never seen her act like this in front of another person before. We lived modestly when she was a child, and it was hard for her to grow up and see that other families didn't look like ours. Somewhere along the way, she shut down. She lived with a piece of herself that felt strange. She has blossomed since moving out here."

Steele looked at her. "I've never met anyone quite like her. She almost never complains. Despite owning her own orchard, she works harder than any 9-5 worker I've ever seen every day. She cares about preserving the past. She loves books, music, and art. She can cook better than my grandmother. May she rest in peace. She is the partner I've been looking for."

"Give her time to digest that. She has chosen partners before knowing they don't matter. You matter to her. That's a new feeling."

He nodded. "I know."

"I hope I see you in many years to come. You make my daughter incredibly happy."

By the time Jovi reentered the room, the subject had shifted to picking a movie that night, and the cinematography of *Avatar* vs. *Titanic* was being heavily debated.

They sat filling the kitchen with laughter. Jovi worked on her fettucine alfredo. She made salads from the garden with the few cucumbers that had started, roasted nuts and a balsamic vinaigrette. She roasted green beans with garlic, and drizzled lemon juice on shrimp then pan fried them with butter. When they ate, they both complimented her with every other bite, Jovi's face flushing. It was a deliciously balanced meal. When they finished, they pulled out a game. The laughter became uncontrollable. Jovi hadn't had this much fun in years.

When they finished, Jovi put on *E.T.* The conversations about movies had much evolved since the previous debate. They were about thirty minutes into the movie when her mom started to doze.

"Can I spend the night?" Steele asked quietly. "I wasn't sure with your mom visiting, but I promise no funny business."

Jovi giggled. "Yes of course you can stay."

Jovi and Steele cuddled, and finished *E.T.* Duchess had long abandoned them to lay by her mom on the other couch. When the movie ended, Jovi turned on the lamp so her Mom could find her way around when she woke up. Then they snuck upstairs quietly, Duchess at their heels. When they crawled in bed, they still hadn't heard her wake up.

"Your mom is pretty awesome." He said.

Jovi looked at him. "Most men think the same."

"That's not what I mean. She is a beautiful woman, but she is clever and very free spirited." Steele said.

Jovi nodded. "She has a very hippie spirit about her. Despite all the rough times she has been through, she still goes with the flow and remains positive and bright. I wish had more of that."

"You have it too." Steele said looking at her. "You see the beauty in everyday surroundings. I've seen you see people right to their cores upon just meeting them. You have been through a lot this summer, and as far as I can tell, it hasn't pushed you off your game at all."

"That's not how I feel like I'm doing." Jovi said. "I feel like I'm letting someone else rule my life."

"You aren't. You are walking through it like it's a minor inconvenience. The only difference between your mom and you is that you are a planner, and she goes with the flow. As a small business owner, you need to be planning, not flowing. As an artist, you need to flow. The difference in your personalities is slight and suites you both. I wouldn't want you to be anyone other than you are." He tenderly kissed her goodnight. "I promised no funny business, but if your mom wasn't here, I'd show you how much I love just the way you are."

She grinned. "Goodnight, Steele."

When her mom got ready to leave Sunday afternoon, it felt too soon. They hugged for what felt like hours. "I don't want you to go." Jovi told her.

"I know, baby. I'll be back to help with opening day. David wouldn't miss it either. It's just over a month away. Let me know if you need me though. I'd be here in a second." She kissed her forehead. "You are doing so well. Tell him. He is one of the good ones."

Chapter 20

The rest of the month flew by like July always does. Jovi worked, ran, and enjoyed nights on her porch. Steele and Hannah had stopped sleeping over nightly, but there hadn't been any problems since. Jovi left snacks for Tori on Tuesdays, and Tori kept patrolling the area. It had gotten dull, and Jovi preferred it that way.

August came, and Steele informed her that he could not possibly give his parents any more excuses about why Jovi couldn't come to dinner this week. So, he was picking her up on Thursday, and she hadn't been this nervous over anything ever.

Thursday evening, Steele came to pick her up. He knew Jovi was nervous, but she was about to be even more nervous. Steele's mom had called his sister who had then called their brother. Steele had not dated since Stacey, and they all knew it. They had all seen them kissing at the Fourth of July, and they knew it was serious. So, this weekly dinner with Mom and Dad turned into a dinner with Emma, her husband, Mike, little Jack, and Christopher. Jovi would be meeting everyone tonight.

"Jovi, are you ready?" Steele asked. He pulled her in and nibbled behind her ear.

Jovi nodded. She had baked an apple pie. It was one of the three desserts out of Lynn's cookbook that she had perfected. She carried it nervously with the bouquet of flowers from her garden. Jovi had picked some of her lavender and zinnias. She hoped Charlene would appreciate the beauty.

"Mom will love these, Jovi. And you look stunning. I need to tell you something before we go so you have time to prepare yourself. I know you need time to process before big steps."

"Steele, I know about your dad's stroke. It doesn't freak me out in the least. I can't wait to meet him. You obviously idolize him." Jovi smiled.

"That's great to hear, but that's not what I mean." He ran his hand through his hair. Jovi wondered why he was nervous. "Everyone is coming, and they insisted on coming. They weren't going to take no for an answer."

"Okay." Jovi said quietly.

"Please don't be afraid. They will love you, and I'll be at your side the whole time. They are just excited, okay?"

Jovi nodded her head and grabbed his hand tight. She did not know this night would end up being a bigger deal than the already big deal it was going to be. She was terrified she would mess this up, but she needed to try to have courage. Lynn had lived her whole life too afraid to love another or tell King exactly what she needed from him. She would not be so afraid of mistakes that she would miss out on her chance with Steele, and that meant meeting the most important people in his life.

Jovi didn't speak the entire way to Steele's childhood home. She held onto his hand like a vice grip. "Don't leave my side. You promised Steele. I didn't grow up with aunts or uncles or siblings. This is all new to me."

"I know, Jovi, but you will do amazing. It's loud and chaotic, but it's people who love each other for always. They want me to be happy, and you do that. Just because you didn't grow up with those people in your life doesn't mean there won't be room for people like that in your life now. It also doesn't mean you won't know how to be around them. You are great with people. Just be yourself."

Jovi clutched her bouquet in one hand and Steele's hand in the other. They opened the door and crossed the threshold into the home. Jovi was with met with the most inviting smells and sounds she had ever experienced. His mother and sister Emma wrapped her in a hug. "Jovi! We are thrilled to finally meet you! Steele has talked about you opening Autumn Gold Orchard next month. We can't wait to come! Jack has never been to an orchard." Jack was the spitting image of his father. He sat on Mike's lap in the living room curiously peaking at the stranger who walked in with his Uncle Steele.

"Hey, buddy!" Steele called to him. "Uncle Steele!" Jack tentatively ran at Steele carefully avoiding Jovi. Steele wrapped him in a hug. Jovi melted. "This is my friend, Jovi. She came her to meet you." Steele said.

Jovi held out her hand. "It's an honor to meet you Jack." Jack shook her hand eyeing her suspiciously. "These are for you." Jovi held out her bouquet to Charlene.

"Your flowers are beautiful, Thank you. I love the smell of lavender. Come in and get comfortable." She ushered Jovi inside.

At the table, Steele's dad, Eddie was a very tall man who looked oversized in his wheelchair. His charming personality made his role as the patriarch of the family clear despite the disabling stroke. "Jovi forgive all the excitement. Everyone has been waiting for Steele to bring you over. To say we are thrilled would be an understatement."

A man stood near Eddie's side. He looked like Steele but was a bit stiffer. He wore a suit and his hair military short. "Jovi. Christopher." He said. They shook hands. "Steele has been stingy with the details. He said I had to meet you to know more. So, I'll need the details from you." He winked. *Did these men all think they were charmers?*

They sat down to eat, and everyone talked almost at once. Emma was a teacher and talked about the play her kids were putting on. Jack always wanted the conversation to be about him, which reminded Jovi of her little brother. Christopher had his fancy job in the city but did hold any air of arrogance about it. He shared about his marathon training and his dating troubles. He couldn't seem to find a woman who suited him. Charlene and Eddie were adorable. Eddie obviously thought Charlene was an actual angel, and he thought she hung the moon. For retiring and Eddie being wheelchair bound, they were still busy bodies who volunteered and frequently visited with friends. Emma's husband Mike had been around long enough that he felt right at home. Although he wasn't as loud as the rest, they shared inside jokes and ganged up on Emma. The atmosphere was inviting, and they all welcomed Jovi like a long-lost daughter. They asked questions about her mother's artwork and what she thought of Steele's most recent facial hair style. Jovi never thought she would leave that night feeling like family.

As night fell, Emma and Mike were the first ones to leave. Jack was up past his bedtime and had started to fuss. "I'm sorry." Emma said. "It's late for him."

"Don't worry about it. Kid's honesty is one of the best things about them." Jovi smiled.

"I'm so happy for you guys, truly." Emma squeezed her tightly with little Jack still in her arms. "Please come back again. Steele deserves to be with a woman can be his equal. I know he has been searching for that and you fit that perfectly." She said quietly.

After Emma's family had left, Jovi and Steele got ready to depart as well. "Remember Jovi, dinner is every Thursday, usually not every hooligan in this family shows up." Eddie smiled.

Jovi laughed. "Goodnight Eddie. Bye Charlene. Nice to meet you Christopher!"

They climbed into Steele's truck. Steele turned his head to face hers, "So?" He asked. "Have they completely scarred you for life?"

"They are wonderful." Jovi replied. "I actually didn't want the night to end." She smiled. "You and your brother both have your father's charisma. You have your mother's steadiness and patience. Christopher isn't quite that way. He looks for immediate results and constant action. He can't sit still for very long. You enjoy sitting still and observing." Jovi said.

"Wow. I knew you were good with people, but bravo. I'll have to be careful where I take you. Maybe we should join a poker group." Steele laughed. "Christopher is a fantastic investment banker because he likes to strike hard and early and see results. Those are the same reasons why he is struggling with women. He sweeps them off their feet only to find out they aren't as enchanting as he thought they were." He glanced at Jovi and then back at the road. "Don't get any ideas. I'm not let down by your enchantments. You are exactly who I thought you were and more. Emma adored you. She has been waiting for a sister in her corner to balance the scales for years." Steele blushed realizing how blunt he had been.

Jovi took his hand. "I liked Emma too." Jovi said confidently.

Steele parked in Jovi's driveway. The sound of crickets and frogs was loud. The stars were on full display. The night was perfect.

"I can't believe how close opening day is getting." Jovi said thoughtfully. "I have apples I am going to be starting to harvest soon. Everything is getting so real."

Steele smiled. "It's going to go off well. You have advertised as much as you could. The place looks great. I'm going to be here as much as you need. Before the season begins and I lose time with you for a few months, I'm taking you ice skating." Jovi laughed. "I love you, Jovi. I want to see this come true for you." Steele said.

Jovi sucked in a breath. "I love you too."

The smile that broke out on Steele's face seemed to start at one ear and end at the other. He wrapped her in a giant bear hug. "That wasn't that scary was it?"

"It feels better to have it out." Jovi said exhaling. "I'll see you later gator." Jovi kissed him and headed inside.

Jovi began harvesting her Duchess apples later that week. She put some in her refrigerators for pre-picked product. She froze some. Then the real work began. She began making canned apple pie filling. She had spent a day with Caroline learning the basics on how to can and was very surprised on how simple it all was. She stuck on a label that she had printed based on Steele's logo and placed them in her orchard barn. When she was satisfied with her apple pie filling, she switched to apple juice. She canned that as well. It was best to have some juice ready to go for cider that season. Jovi started to assemble her pies based on Lynn's recipe and stuck the pies in the freezer. For days, her routine consisted of running, and spending the early morning in the garden, harvesting apples, and the afternoon was spent preparing them.

Jovi was in kitchen working on her pies. She had been in there for hours. At this point, it felt like she had been making pie filling for days. Steele walked in, and. Jovi looked up at him, and saw him, but her mind went blank. *What day was it? Was he supposed to be here? Had she forgotten something?*

"Jovi, love, you look like a zombie. Have you eaten today? Put that down. I'll finish this. You go shower and change, I'm taking you out." He grabbed the rolling pin out of her hands gently.

"I can't go out. I need to finish these." She looked frantic. He was right though; she hadn't eaten today.

"Jovi, I'm looking at about 50 pies right in front of me. I'm sure you have tons more done and hidden away. Let me stick these in the freezer and finish this one up. You need to take a break before you enter opening day already worn out."

Jovi let out a huge exhale and her shoulders slumped. Steele was right. She was exhausted. She looked around her kitchen. It looked like a bomb had gone off.

He saw her looking. "I'll get that too. Go clean up. Take your time."

When Jovi looked at herself in the mirror while the shower warmed, she instantly started laughing. Her hair was a complete mess, and it was covered in flour. Her shirt was stained from pie filling and her make-up was smeared everywhere from the heat of the kitchen. She through her clothes in the hamper and got in the shower. She stood there until she felt the life come back into her.

She wasn't sure where Steele was taking her, but a favorite pair of jeans and a flattering reliable shirt was the most reliable outfit of choice. She came down the stairs a new woman. She peered into her kitchen to see a spotless room. Steele had put away all of her pies. The counter tops were clean. The dishwasher was running. And she could see him at the sink cleaning her giant bowls and rolling pins. It was the sexiest thing she had ever seen. He turned around and grinned. "Are you ready?"

She nodded. "Yes, much better. Thank you."

Chapter 21

Steele picked up a pizza and they headed to a part of town Jovi hadn't explored yet. A large building that looked like a shed with a big parking lot came into view. They parked. There was a sign in front Woodsburrow Ice Arena. She looked at him. "We are going skating?" He nodded. He grabbed the pizza and Jovi's hand. They went inside.

There were a few other people there, but it was very quiet. Jovi and Steele found a table and opened up the box that held their pizza with the works. Jovi ate half the pizza herself. As she grabbed her last piece, she looked at Steele. "I haven't been eating. I'm nervous and the days seem to be over before I remember to make something." She said

He nodded. "I figured. Your text messages started to make very little sense." He pulled out a box and set it on the table.

Jovi opened it. Beautiful baby blue skates were inside. They were her size. "Steele, thank you! These are almost too pretty to wear. I really am not that good." She looked at him.

"You will need a pair. Put them on. I'll give you a refresher."

They skated for the next two hours. Jovi wasn't half bad, but she did end up with a sore butt from falling hard a few times. She could see Steele's confidence and excitement on the ice. It was as playful as she had seen him be. Jovi looked forward to seeing more sides of him. The more she learned, the more she loved about him. He kissed her in the middle of the rink after everyone had gone home. She felt like a princess. He locked up the rink and took her home. It was a magical evening and just what Jovi needed.

***

When Jovi had one week until opening day, her excitement was growing. She felt like a kid expecting the arrival of Christmas. She had other varieties of apples that were starting to ripen. She had hung her lights and made sure the orchard was tidy and accessible. She had begun bringing pumpkins up to her prepicked pumpkin patch. Pumpkins sat in long rows. She was impressed with how many had grown. There should be enough to sell throughout the entire season. She had her temporary staff, which was mostly high school kids, come in one afternoon so she could run down expectations on what a shift would look like. She had a great group of kids who were excited and respectable. She had snatched up a few of Steele's hockey players, and some of her fellow farmer's kids. She made them all feel welcome, and they all gave her 100%.

Opening day was scheduled for Saturday, September 1st. Her mom and David were expected to arrive on Thursday night to help her prepare the day before. Hannah had promised to be there on Friday to help with baking. Steele had taken the entire week off and had already been there every day to be at her beck and call, and to make sure she was getting fed. *How had she gotten so lucky?* On Wednesday evening, Steele and Jovi went to bed satisfied that preparations were going better than they had expected, but around midnight that night, her security cameras alerted. Jovi had had a few animals alert her over the last month, so she slowly rolled over to check the camera., When she pulled up the system however, she didn't see any animals. What she saw and heard, were flames.

The hay wagon was parked right up against the barn and the flames coming out of the center grew larger, and Jovi let out a large gasp followed by a scream. Steele bolted up and leaned over. "Call 911 Jovi." He said. He threw on some pants and ran outside. Jovi called. The dispatch said the fire department and an officer would be out in the next fifteen minutes. Jovi pocketed her phone and ran out after Steele. Steele was hosing down the hay wagon as much as he could.

When the fire department arrived, they put out the fire completely. Thankfully, the hay wagon had been the only loss. If any second had been longer in that process, the entire barn would have been gone. The responding firefighter seemed certain the fire had been started intentionally. Jovi was angry, and she had had enough. She grabbed an old spotlight that was obnoxiously bright and walked around the wagon behind the back of the barn. On the ground in an area that had been recently stepped on, was a shiny large bracelet. "Tori!" She called. "Come see this!"

Tori jogged over to join her. "Have you ever seen that before?" Tori asked.

Jovi shook her head no. "I haven't been back to this side of the barn in weeks either. There is a path here that looks like someone trampled on the grass recently."

Tori very carefully picked up the bracelet as Steele left his conversation with the firefighter to amble over. "I know that bracelet." He said.

Jovi looked at him confused. "You do?"

He nodded. "Nancy has worn that bracelet since Stacey was in high school."

Tori examined the bracelet and sure enough, on the wrist side there was an engraving. *To the most glamorous woman I'll ever know. -Rich* "Well," said Tori. "Time to make some uncomfortable waves. I'll have some tough questions for the most glamorous woman in town. I will be in touch."

Steele grabbed Jovi in a side hug. "How am I going to fix this before Saturday? What did I do to make the woman that has everything hate me this much?" Jovi asked as tears started to run down her cheeks.

"Jovi, this isn't on you. Let's let Tori do her job and go inside."

Jovi took a long shower when they got back in the house. She needed to get some rest because tomorrow would be a huge day, but it was 3:00 AM and she was waiting to hear those magic words from Tori. She had enough of this torture. She crawled into bed and laid there with her eyes open as Steele rubbed her back. Then, a text message. *We got her. I'll send Luke by in the morning. There will be no more vandalism. Get some sleep.* "Yes!" Jovi exclaimed. She felt the anxiety wash away and with it, the adrenaline she had been feeling all night. They drifted off to sleep.

Luke arrived around 8:00 AM to tell her what they had discovered. "Tori found her at the local hospital. She was trying to claim she had burnt her had cooking dinner that evening and was unable to sleep, but the fire that she started caught onto the gloves she thought were clever to wear. She had taken it off and threw it onto the hay wagon. She lost her bracelet in the process. She gave us no indication on why she committed those crimes and denied it. There is no doubt in my mind she is guilty." Luke said. "We got her."

Jovi gave Luke a giant hug. "It's over, and with not a minute to spare. I have two days until opening day."

"I'll be over with Hannah tomorrow to help how I can. I'm sure this will be all over town as well."

Jovi groaned. "Great. Nothing like the gossip mill."

"I'll see you guys tomorrow." Luke said.

"Later Luke."

They said goodbye and their bro hug was longer than it usually was. Jovi knew they had been anxiously wanting an arrest as well.

Jovi and Steele went outside to survey the damage. The wagon was a goner. She would have to buy a new one, but there were only a few days until opening day. This wasn't the time to wagon shop. Looking around, everything else seemed to be in order. It appeared that Nancy had begun to smash pumpkins, but after a couple it must have been too difficult to accomplish. Jovi's pumpkins were large, and Nancy was a tiny woman. They picked up the remnants of the smashed few and replaced them with a few new ones.

Jovi called the Grants and told them about the further damage and the arrest of Nancy Webster. "I never liked her." Caroline replied. "I'm so relieved they caught her. We have been worried sick about you all summer. What can we do to help?"

"I was hoping Charlie might have a wagon that we could use here for the season." Jovi said. Jovi could hear her call to Charlie on the other end of the line. Charlie mumbled something back that Jovi couldn't hear.

"We are on our way." Caroline said, and she hung up.

Jovi looked at Steele. "I guess Caroline and Charlie are coming over." Steele smiled. "This town has it bad for you." Jovi laughed.

Caroline and Charlie arrived within the hour, pulling a hay wagon that although would be small for harvesting hay in the present day, was absolutely perfect for hayrides. They had filled it with hay for sitting on. "This wagon originally was used with the tractor that you have. When Lynn bought the tractor, she didn't want the wagon. She purchased a new one. This has been sitting on our property. We don't use it. It's too small for the harvesting that we need to do. It's yours, kid." Charlie said.

Jovi wrapped a hug around him. "Thank you, Charlie. You are the hero of the day."

He smiled at her. "We are so proud of you." Charlie hooked up the hay wagon and parked it, so it was exactly where he wanted it Saturday. Jovi showed him the route. Charlie reminded her to get some extra gas, and Caroline and Charlie checked out the barn, the pumpkins, and the orchard. "You did a fantastic job, Jovi. People will love it." They said to her. "We will be here bright and early Saturday. We are hoping you get a great turn out. You deserve it." They hugged and the Grants left. The nerves started to set in.

Chapter 22

Steele and Jovi stopped for lunch, or maybe it was brunch. She couldn't remember what time it was today, and Steele had just been bringing her food according to his internal clock. As they sat on the patio, Duchess began to bark at an approaching car. A Mercedes that seemed flash "Expensive!" to everyone that saw, pulled into the driveway. Steele stood as Richard emerged. He walked up to the porch as a low growl grew in Duchess' throat. "Jovi? My name is Richard. I think we have some talking to do. I owe you an apology." Jovi gestured at the chair to her left, and they sat down.

"A long time ago," Richard began "I was in love with a woman. She was radiant and strong. I couldn't imagine anyone being as lovely as she was. I met her working at my parent's construction business. We would sneak off where no one knew and spend time together. My parents had insisted for years that I had to marry a client's daughter. We did a lot of construction for big businesses, although that wasn't the only type we did. They wanted me to have a life that was easier than the one they lead. It was important to them that I was comfortable, respected. The woman I was in love with, had no social standing and came with no money to her name. I knew they wouldn't approve, so I hid our relationship, from everyone. Not long after our affair had begun, she was pregnant. It was my time to man up and stand up to my family for the one that I was creating. I loved this woman, and this was my baby. I had made that baby aware and was old enough to understand the consequences. I couldn't leave them stranded without me because I couldn't be a man to my parents and tell them what I really wanted. That night when I got home, they told me they had arranged a date for me with Nancy. Her family owned the hotel in town and was expanding it to another. I tried to tell them I didn't want to date her, but the words wouldn't come out. Not long after, the woman I loved miscarried the baby. The woman was heartbroken, and I felt like it was my fault. I had caused her so much stress keeping our relationship hidden that killed our baby."

Tears rolled down his cheeks from the pain he still felt at the loss years later. "My parents expected a proposal, so by the winter, Nancy and I were married. She knew I never loved her. We had one child, because that was what was expected of us, and I never ended my affair. I loved that woman. Lynn was the love of my life, and I treated her so unfairly. She was worth much more than a secret closet romance. Nancy was terribly jealous. I never told her, but we have been married long enough, eventually she discovered who the woman was. When Lynn died, Nancy was relieved to have that piece gone, but then you moved into town. You put that picture in the paper of Lynn and I in the orchard and started seeing Steele. It was more than Nancy could take. She isn't strong like you and Lynn. In the end, all of this is my fault. I full intend to pay for the damage, and I'd like to make a large donation in Lynn's name. Autumn Gold was the only thing in life that Lynn cared about. I'd like to make sure that continues for her in death. He handed her a check that more than covered the damage and distress that Lynn had caused. It also insured without a doubt, there would be another season at Autumn Gold.

"I think you were a coward, Richard." He bowed his head. "I'm very sorry for your loss though. Losing Lynn and holding it inside must have been soul crushing." He looked up at her, confused by the kindness she was showing him. "You are welcome to revisit her memory any time here at Autumnn Gold."

They shook hands, and he left. Steele stared at her dumbfounded. "You never cease to amaze me."

Jovi gave him a grin. "My mom and David will be here soon. Let's finish up."

***

The next 24 hours were a blur to Jovi. Her family arrived right on time. David helped set up the cashier area. Her mom brought the most gorgeous paintings. She had done a set of ten in varying sizes. They were all of different areas she could identify on her property some were up very close with apples blown up in a proportion double its regular size and some were zoomed out, like the view of the woods from the trail. They were magnificent, and Steele and Luke had hung them all on a side wall. "There is one more I made for you." Her mom pulled out a canvas that was smaller than the ones that had been hung. It was of Jovi and Steele in an embrace as Jovi laughed in front of the orchard in her driveway. The colors that swirled around them made them look like they were being swept up. It was magnificent and showed Jovi's feelings for Steele in a tangible way.

"Wow Mom." She hugged her mom whose belly was expanding almost daily it seemed. She was still in good spirits though and seemed to glide along instead of the waddle that pregnant woman usually did at that stage.

Hannah baked feverishly in the kitchen and made cider doughnuts, apple muffins, apple strudel and cycled Jovi's pies into the oven. She made a giant vat of caramel that would be on in the miniature baking house. The employees would make caramel apples on demand out there. Besides the caramel apples, they would be offering apple cider and fresh doughnuts to be made every few hours to keep the smell of the yeasted goodies in the air.

That night, Jovi had a bonfire with all the hands that helped that day. Surrounding her in a circle was her mom with her little brother curled on her lap, David, Hannah, Luke, Steele, and the Grants that had stopped by with some mums and sunflowers to add some flair to the space and had never left. She was surrounded by the people who made her, her. These people made this day possible. She felt loved, grateful, and whole.

September 1st started with a cool morning. It was as if mother nature knew what they needed was some fall weather. Autumn Gold was set to open at 11:00, and Jovi was terrified no one would show. She had been hanging fliers and advertising for weeks. The orchard was immaculate. There were varieties ready to harvest for the pick your own. The River Runners were set to perform from noon to four. The Fat Hippo was bringing their truck there for the day. She hoped bringing them would pay off. Charlie had the tractor ready to go for rides, and Steele and Luke had started the bonfire and made some signs showing visitors the trails and where to go. Hannah was running the miniature bakery. They only thing left to do, was remember to breathe, and hope that customers would come.

At 11:00 cars started to come with voracity and didn't slow until closing. The first people who arrived, were Steele's entire family. They gave her giant hugs and huge congratulations. Jovi introduced them to her family, and they bought more than they could carry. She watched little Jack get his photo taken next to the giant metal apple tree Steele had made. People started to cover the property everywhere. The wagon rides were full. Pictures were taken at the photo area. Caramel apples made sticky hands. At the end of the day, Jovi was sold out of prepicked apples. She was left with very little artisan items; she had already contacted all of the people she had displayed items for, and all were bringing everything they had the next morning. She had heard stories about Lynn's time at the orchard and felt like she had been there today. To see all the people, she loved coming together in one space was amazing. As night fell, the folk band left, as did the BBQ truck and the lights came on around the bonfire. The men lit the hike down into the woods.

"Can I steal you?" Steele pulled on her arm.

Jovi looked around. Everything seemed to be going without a hitch, there wasn't much she needed to do any more. People were gathered around the fire. Her mom and little brother were already asleep in the house. "Yeah, you can." She said distractedly smiling at him.

He grabbed her hand, and they walked out of the crowd. "First things first." He pulled out a bag of her favorite pulled pork sandwich and handed her a cup of apple cider.

How did he always know to do that? She ate and felt grateful she hadn't missed out on the dish that had inspired her to invite The Fat Hippo in the first place. It was delicious. When she was done, he took her hand. "Let's go for a walk." They followed the glow of lights into the woods until they reached the bench that Steele had made. They sat in the silence.

"This day has been perfect." Jovi said smiling into the night. "Can you believe how busy we were?" She saw Steele shift beside her. He pulled out a tiny box.

"Almost perfect." He spoke. "Jovi, meeting you this year has been the best thing that has ever happened to me. I love you, and this place, and I can't imagine being anywhere else. Will you marry me?"

Jovi glanced down at the ring that was a vintage style, tiny diamonds covered the ring with intricate details. "Yes." She whispered before she even knew what she was saying. *Had she just agreed to be his wife?* Holy cow her brain was on fire.

He slipped the ring on her finger when she realized the ring wasn't just vintage style, it was vintage. "It was my grandmother's." Steele said. "She would have loved you."

Jovi sat there with Steele, and the ring that sat heavily on her finger marking its permanent presence on her. She felt rooted and complete. This was the place she was meant to be.

Meet the author

J.R. Cook is a wife and mom who has been a lover of books since she could read. She has a great love for all things UpNorth, and making the world a more beautiful place to be.

www.ingramcontent.com/pod-product-compliance
Lightning Source LLC
Chambersburg PA
CBHW031533310726

48971CB00008B/2467